Shifti

The Salvation of Tempestria
Book 1

Gary Stringer

First paperback edition December 2020

Cover Design by BespokeBookCovers.com

ISBN 978-1-8382777-0-3 (Paperback)
ISBN 978-1-8382777-1-0 (eBook)

Published by Gary Stringer

www.amazon.co.uk/Shifting-Stars-Gary-Stringer/dp/1838277706

www.goodreads.com/book/show/56856086-shifting-stars

Chapter 1

My name is Arshes Megane and I present this in defence of my actions. As I write this, at my behest, Aunt Mandalee has already gone to fetch my father from a critical moment, a thousand years ago. I understand that this Time Intervention is illegal and dangerous. Potentially catastrophic. Yet, I maintain I am right to do this. To me, the choice is simple: sit here, meekly playing by the rules while the world burns, or throw the rulebook on the fire and save...everything. Or try to.

But I'm getting ahead of myself, or possibly behind myself. That's the trouble with Time manipulation: it can be hard to tell. Either way, let me take a step back, or forward, take a breath and begin to compose myself.

The moon is but a silver sliver in a starry sky, as I gaze out of my window. Hence, my desk is littered with lighted candles aplenty and an oil lamp for extra illumination on this page. Of course, I could simply speak a word of magic and light up this room as brightly as if it were Midsummer's Day. Indeed, in this age of magical wonders, there are commonplace spells with which I could transfer my thoughts directly onto magical recording devices. But tonight is not a night for magic.

These days, there is a small but vocal group of individuals who believe we have become lazy in this modern age and desensitised to the non-magical wonders that have surrounded us for who knows how long. Aunt Dreya would call that 'sentimental nonsense.' For her, magic is all; even more so since Ascending to the higher planes. Oh, how I miss her!

Me? I take a more balanced view of magic. While I appreciate its place in the world and all we can do, tonight, as I say, is not a night for magic. So, I sit at my desk, armed with nothing more than a pen and inscribe the words onto paper, as it was done in ages past – simpler times, when the dew of Creation was still fresh upon the world.

Please, gentle reader, forgive my ramblings. I sometimes get so caught up in the simple pleasures of this form of non-magical creativity that I forget what it is I am supposed to be writing about. For the record, allow me to introduce myself: I am the only daughter of Daelen

StormTiger and Catriona Redfletching. These are names that are remembered with honour in times past, present and, I trust, in the future as well, if you will forgive such crude temporal terms. In case there is ever such a time that the old legends fade and are forgotten, however, let me write further.

My name is Arshes Megane and I am immortal.

Perhaps I should have led with that, but there's a fine line between dramatic and pretentious.

When I say immortal, I do not mean merely long-lived, but nor should you imagine that immortality is the same as omniscience or invulnerability, though I do possess unique powers and natural defences that I use to protect myself and those I care about. Immortality means that my ageing process stopped more than nine centuries ago and will never restart, leaving me with the appearance of a young woman of around nineteen or twenty. Barring some grand cosmic accident, or unless I fulfil my final destiny, whatever that might be, I shall exist until the end of eternity. Does eternity have an end, or does it go on forever? I do not know. Moreover, it occurs to me that true immortality is something that cannot be proven. Who but another immortal could be around to verify it? Philosophy aside, however, proof or not, I know that it is true.

How this came to be, I cannot say. A consequence of being born within the Guardianship? The Guardians exist out of Time, and I am so far the only child to be born in its embrace. A legacy of my father? He did originate from one of the higher planes of existence, where Time flows differently. Heritage from my mother's Faery blood? To the Faery of Quarthonia, I am Emryse Amrosia – Ever-Living – the latest of several immortals that feature in song and story, if one is to believe such things. (As a corollary to my earlier musings, I can't help but wonder, if there have been other immortals before, why have I not met them? By definition, they must be alive somewhere!) Maybe it is a combination of all these factors. Perhaps it is none of them. Once again, whatever the reason, all I know is that it is true: My name is Arshes Megane, and I am immortal.

Accepting this fact, you will appreciate that I have a unique perspective on the world. That is why I am sitting here, preparing to write this story: no other could.

I am choosing to call these ramblings, 'The Salvation of Tempestria' in desperate hopes that events yet to come will match the title. If anything goes wrong – perhaps the smallest mistake – then as far as this world, this reality is concerned, the events I relate to you will never happen. Yet I swear to you on all I hold sacred – by the memory of my father, through the love of my mother, on the very essence of magic itself – that every word I write is true.

But I am in danger of starting my story at the end instead of the middle. I understand it is customary to start a story at the beginning, but when one lives outside Time as I do, the beginning can sometimes be…elusive. Besides, sometimes, unless the middle happens as it's supposed to, the beginning may never happen. So, gentle reader, allow me to present the Salvation of Tempestria, in the middle.

*****

As I gaze through Time to that moment, gentle reader, I can see that Daelen has agreed that it would be best to camp for one more night and begin the final push to Kullos' fortress at first light. Since there are no more plans to make, while the others head for their tents for the night, the shadow warrior has chosen to go for a walk alone to relax. He knows it will probably be his last chance to enjoy something so simple.

Even with all his power, the great shadow warrior always took pleasure in the smallest things.

That is a side to my father that people often do not appreciate. Perhaps it is his influence, as much as my mother's, that compels me to write this story in such an archaic manner as ink inscribed onto paper with a pen.

The shadow warrior has been walking for close to an hour, when he comes across a female figure standing in the moonlight, dressed in white body armour much like his own, with white boots and a purple mask that conceals the upper part of her face.

"Greetings, Daelen," she offers. "Ah, but it is good to see you like this again; it's been a while."

I can see he recognises her. Almost. Something about her causes Daelen's memory to flashback to when his current mission all started. She looks very different, but somehow, her aura is the same.

"You're her, aren't you?" he says, at last. "You're the one who woke me from my rest and made me aware of the threat and the power of Kullos in the first place. Who are you?"

Considering how to answer without revealing too much too soon, her mouth twitches as a very old memory flashes through her mind. A thousand years ago from her perspective. Just a few days from his.

"You once referred to me as an Assassin Peacemaker," she replies at last.

"Mand—?"

"—Don't say my name!" his visitor cuts him off. "You don't know what terrible trouble you could cause. That's why I didn't use it myself. You asked who I am, and now you know, but I'm not who you think I am…or maybe I am, in a way, but never mind, there will be time for explanations later. Assuming there still is a later. Right now, I need your help."

Ever stubborn, Daelen wants some answers right then and there.

"But how can you be here?" he demands. "When I left, you were asleep back there!"

"Oh, don't worry, I still am," is her reply, "and I'm not here…that is, rather, I am here, but you are not. Yes, well, it's a bit difficult to explain, really."

Ah, gentle reader, that is so typical of my dear Aunt Mandalee, the White Assassin. She often said she dearly wished these things weren't so hard to explain. Even now, I know she sometimes wonders if she makes any sense at all. She's too hard on herself. She never chose to be a diplomat, a teacher or a politician. She became a demon hunter, an assassin and a Cleric of Nature. How strange it is that she is the only one of the original Three Guardians still in the position, at least she was until she agreed to this desperate act. I'm sure any rational person would have placed wagers on her being the first to resign. Of course, one wonders what exactly counts as reason in this irrational world, but that, gentle reader, is a subject better suited to my philosophy texts. For now, I have a story to tell.

"Look, if you'll just come with me a little way further into the woods, we'll be able to speak more freely."

"Alright," Daelen agrees and extends his arm for Aunt Mandalee to take as they stroll along.

She smiles at the gesture. It's a rather old-fashioned tradition, from her perspective, but she can see no harm in indulging him.

*****

After walking for no more than five minutes, the woodland opens out into a clearing and Mandalee declares that they have arrived.

Releasing her hold on Daelen's arm, she at last removes her mask so he can see her face. A face that appears about ten years older than when he last saw her an hour ago.

"You're from the future!" Daelen realises. "You're a future M–." He catches himself. "A future version of the woman I know."

Mandalee pulls a face.

"That is a very crude description, Daelen. The reality has to do with the true nature of Time and its relative spatial dimensions, but I can't tell you about that."

"Why not?"

"You're not ready for it. Your entire home plane of existence isn't ready for it yet."

"Are you really so advanced in your time?" Daelen breathes in awe, trying to imagine a future where the knowledge of mere mortals might surpass that of his people. It's hard for him to imagine how such a thing is possible.

"Yes," Mandalee agrees, "as a matter of fact, we are. In some ways, at least."

"If you are so advanced, how come you need help from someone as primitive and backward as me?"

"Now, now, Daelen. Be nice," Mandalee chides him gently.

"Sorry," Daelen apologises. "That was uncalled for, wasn't it?"

"Yes, actually, it was. To answer the essence of your question, though…well, for now, let's just say the danger we face is unique to your own experience. Will you help us?"

Daelen gazes around the clearing in which he is standing. It surely reminds him of Catriona's Meadow, except he knows it's entirely the wrong world for that. He feels there's something else about it, something strange – it's been nagging him since he first entered, but he can't put his finger on what it is. That's making him irritable and stubborn.

"In case you've forgotten your history, I'm in the middle of something important right now."

"Not from my perspective, you're not," Mandalee counters. "Look, if you help us and we succeed, I shall return you but a moment after we left, and you can get back to fighting Kullos. It won't affect you in any way."

"And if we fail?" Daelen asks, fearing the answer he knows is coming.

"If we fail, my friend, nothing you do here will matter."

"It doesn't seem like I have much choice," the shadow warrior grumbles.

"Of course you have a choice," Mandalee counters. "But within the parameters of who you are, I agree – there's no other you could make."

"You've changed," Daelen observes.

The assassin shrugs. "Happens to the best of us, dear."

*****

He couldn't have failed to notice how evasive she is, and there's a casual flippancy in her voice that the Mandalee he knows would never have used. The Mandalee he knows is a throw-caution-to-the-wind young woman who often uses 'get very drunk, armed to the teeth and go for it' as the way to catch her mark. What Daelen doesn't know is that for so long, she has been the White Guardian, not the White Assassin and that has led her to adapt.

Living outside Time, she has aged no more than ten years in the traditional sense, due to accumulated days within the Timestream. Even so, one day, a few years ago, when I asked her how she was truly feeling, she admitted to me, "I feel old."

As an immortal, gentle reader, I am beginning to understand what she meant.

After she has assisted me with this Illegal Time Intervention, she has vowed to resign from the Guardianship, both in protest at the others' refusal to act and, as she put it, "Because it's time," which is a strange concept for one who lives outside Time, but I could see the sense of it.

Take it from one who knows: Timelessness is wearying.

If all goes well, Mandalee will return to the timestream to live out the rest of her natural human life. It is my hope and my prayer that she will recapture her youth and rejoin the hunt. When I project that possible future, the early signs are promising. Her feline friend Shyleen's coat seems to already have a new glossy golden sheen to it, as well.

Yes, no doubt her resignation is the best thing for her, even though I know it means I will lose her as I have lost everyone else.

As I have said, I am not merely Timeless; I am immortal. I just wonder, gentle reader: how exactly does one resign from immortality?

*****

Accepting her plea for help, Daelen says, "Alright, are you going to open the portal, or shall I?"

"Portal?" Mandalee looks amused.

"Yes, you know, to travel to your time."

"Portal?" she repeats, laughing despite the seriousness of the situation. "My goodness, how quaint! I'm almost tempted to let you do it, just for the experience, but now is not the time for such crude techniques. We don't use portals anymore, my friend."

"Then how do we get to your time?"

With a smile, she replies, "We're already here."

"That's why this place feels strange! I've walked through this forest so many times, and I don't remember ever noticing this place before."

"That's because it doesn't exist," Mandalee explains.

"You mean, it doesn't exist in my time?"

"It doesn't exist in any time."

"Then, where are we?" Daelen looks confused. "I mean, this ground we're standing on, where is it?"

Mandalee sighs; exasperated. "It's nowhere! I told you – it doesn't exist!"

Poor Mandalee. It's like trying to explain the Origin of the Universe to a baby. Daelen is simply not sufficiently developed to cope with it. So many of what are considered the most basic root concepts are beyond anything the shadow warrior has had to deal with, and Mandalee has neither the time nor the patience to take him through nursery education.

Trying to rationalise it, Daelen asks, "Are you saying this glade is an illusion?"

"Oh no, it's real; it just doesn't exist. Look, it all comes down to the manipulation of spatial dynamics and dimensional harmonics to annexe a section of spacetime. This place is special because it's Timeless, but similar annexes are routinely created. It's simple enough – delicate and intricate, but not hard. Any other questions?"

"Just one, about Time travel: you act as if it's commonplace."

"It is," she replies.

"Since when?"

"For the Guardians, from their creation – it's a natural consequence of existing out of Time. For the members of the Higher Council, over a century. For your average wizards, druids and clerics, about half that time. Then in recent years, basic observation-only Time travel has been available to all for recreation, vacations and study."

"That's impossible!" Daelen insists. He's obviously finding it very hard to adjust to a world that has left him behind. "I would have noticed! Where are all these travellers from the future? Why aren't they all over the place? Why haven't I met any, apart from you?"

"Oh, the arrogance!" Mandalee rolls her eyes. "I had almost forgotten that about you. I often used to wonder if the real reason you left your plane of existence was that your ego grew too large and it just sort of spilt out like an overfilled bathtub. The reason you haven't met any other Time travellers is that, except for the Guardians, nobody has ever gone back this far."

"Why not?"

"Because, my dear shadow warrior, you're just not interesting enough yet. Now, if you're quite finished, it's time for us to join a friend of mine so she can explain the current situation. She is looking forward to seeing you."

With that, the White Guardian flies into the air, leaving Daelen little choice but to follow meekly behind.

*****

Lying is generally frowned upon by White Clerics, but I'm sure all the gods of goodness will forgive Aunt Mandalee for her taking sweet revenge for how the shadow warrior had acted so superior and condescending when they first met. Surely, in that context, no-one could blame her for this harmless bit of fun.

I'm sure, gentle reader, you will have noticed, that she used the phrase 'observation-only.' That's because the real answer to Daelen's question is that the magic used for mass-market Time travel necessarily makes the visitors completely invisible and incorporeal to the natives of that time. Only the Guardians and I have Interactive Time travel, which is why only Mandalee could visit Daelen in this way and enlist his much-needed help.

Now that he's agreed, I can get on with my story, secure in the knowledge that my plans are in motion, metaphorically speaking. Literally speaking, *nothing* is in motion, because I'm keeping my house frozen in what I suppose one might call a bubble of Time.

In another quirk of my unique magio-physiology, I can create a Time travel dead zone around me, which I can extend to those nearby. That's how I'm holding the Black and Red Guardians captive in my room, so they can't interfere with what Mandalee is doing. Effectively, I have changed the Time settings to 'observation only' so that I can see and relate a first-hand account of what happened in what one might crudely call the past. The two Guardians can't stop me, because – and I say this without conceit – they're not powerful enough without the 'Power of Three.' And, before you say anything, yes, I know that's a cliché, and no, they don't really call it that. I just say it to wind them up and prick their egos a bit.

Nevertheless, the point still stands: The Guardians are greater than the sum of their parts, which is why it's so sad to see them divided like this. It is my hope that the story I write will convince them, the Council, and you, gentle reader, that I am doing the right thing.

'Who keeps me in check?' you may ask.

Why, Aunt Mandalee, of course! If ever I am on the receiving end of one of her Looks of Disappointment, I am completely powerless. No magic required. And failing her, there's always Shyleen. You might not know it to see the leopard as she is now, curled up by my fire and beginning to purr, but trust me: that is one cat you don't want to cross!

In case you haven't guessed, the 'friend' Mandalee is bringing Daelen to see, is me. I suppose it was easier for her to go with the word 'friend' rather than 'immortal daughter from your future, a product of a relationship you never even got to have and who, if things go wrong between you and Catriona before they're supposed to go wrong, might never exist, but no pressure.'

It will be strange to meet him, when for nearly a thousand years I've believed I would never have a chance to know him.

But my special relationship with Time is relevant for another reason. Even though from an external frame of reference, the pair will be here any moment, I still have as much time as I need to write this story. I know it's weird, but as Mandalee so eloquently put it: The explanation has to do with the true nature of Time and its relative spatial dimensions, but I can't tell you about that because you're not ready for it.

No offence.

Actually, I am doing you a favour by not telling you how it works; I know exactly how it works, and the whole thing makes my head hurt. I wouldn't want to inflict that on all my innocent readers, so in short, it's best to stick with the image of a bubble in Time.

Now, I think it's high time I gave you some much-needed perspective on my mother, Catriona, and my two Aunts, Mandalee and Dreya. The people who made me who I am and the world what it is. To do that, I must take us back to the beginning…

…Or, at least, an earlier part of the middle.

Chapter 2

The world of Tempestria was well-named, for the sky, both day and night, was dominated by a perpetual vortex of swirling energy. The shape and pattern were continually shifting, and its intensity seemed to wax and wane according to some vast cosmic cycle, but even at its lowest ebb, it was far from what anyone could describe as 'calm.' Of course, in those days, no-one in this world considered this unusual or strange. After all, they knew of no other worlds with which to compare theirs. To the people of Tempestria, this was simply the nature of reality.

Now and then a group would spring up, claiming that the world had not always been so and that it had once had another name entirely. Depending on prevailing social attitudes, the response to these individuals ranged from polite sympathy for their delusional state through to, I'm sorry to say, gentle reader, persecution and violence.

Catriona was born to parents who many considered mismatched. Her father, Gabrian, was one of the long-lived Faery who was as rooted to his sun-drenched Quarthonian forest as any oak tree. Like many Faery, he grew uncomfortable if he strayed too far from his forest home. The one time he visited a human city, he became seriously ill. While not as ancient as many of the Quarthonian trees, at almost two hundred years old, he was considered middle-aged. Gabrian was a druid mage, a healer in the community, while Catriona's mother, Velena Redfletching, was a fierce warrior. Equally adept at hunting both animals and people, she was well-known for the battle frenzy that would come upon her when she felt threatened. This greatly enhanced her speed, strength and focus, to the point where nothing could sway, divert or reason with her. Aged just nineteen when she first met Gabrian, she was more at home in the crowded city streets at night and rarely stayed in one place for long. She was indeed the unstoppable force to Gabrian's immovable object. The name Redfletching came from Velena's trademark ruby-coloured feathers, which adorned the tails of all her arrows. Catriona adopted the practice and earned the name on the day she outshot her mother.

Despite their differences – or perhaps because of them – Gabrian and Velena were hopelessly attracted to each other. Catriona was the fruit of their love, their only child. Trained in the formidable archery and hunting skills of her mother and the gentle magic of her father as she grew up, she proved to be highly gifted in both sides. From a young age, she appreciated the strength that is found in diversity and committed herself to the pursuit of Balance in herself, in magic and in the world.

Outwardly, modern-day Faery were slightly smaller than the average human and considerably lighter, possessing hollow bones as a legacy of evolution from creatures that could fly. Faery did not have wings, however, and depictions of winged Faery were generally deemed offensive. Their most distinctive feature was a stripe of small brown spots that ran down each side of their body, legs and arms. Catriona's markings extended to her face, although as a half-Faery, they were faded, so they could easily be mistaken for freckles. Cat was always quick to make it clear that they were not.

The mortals of Tempestria shared their world with higher planar beings, powerful even beyond the gods to whom they prayed. Every now and then, Daelen StormTiger would drop out of the sky and fight some unfathomable cosmic threat known as Kullos, and often their great and terrible battles took their toll on innocent Tempestrians. According to legend, one particularly devastating battle, in ages past, caused Daelen to somehow split in two. He and his twin, generally known as the dark clone, did not get on, and so Daelen had two nemeses to fight. Relative to my mother's time, that was a thousand years ago and even now, almost a thousand beyond that, we know almost nothing about the world before that time. There are no records, no history books. Nothing. To all intents and purposes, that was Year Zero, but that's clearly impossible.

All mortals knew of Daelen was that he was something called a shadow warrior – as was Kullos – a being of incredible power and their world's self-styled protector. It was a matter of some debate as to whether the world would, in fact, need a protector if he would simply go away, which, to the relief of many, he did for long periods. Still, nobody, not even the wizards and the clerics, had the power to do much about it when Daelen StormTiger chose to return and 'protect' them once more.

*****

At first, the attack on Catriona's village seemed just another unfortunate site of these cosmic battles. Daelen appeared, as he always did, in the middle of a violent storm, bringing thunder, rain and lightning flashes that seemed to be shaped in the image of a great tiger. But there was something different about this attack: this time Kullos appeared to have an ally, which was unheard of. An ally who seemed intent on razing their quiet little village to the ground, as if in revenge for some terrible affront or unknowable offence they had caused.

The village was not entirely alone in the face of this supernatural force. The Champion of the Gods, the faithful companion of Daelen StormTiger, was with them. He was called Ossian Miach Kaidool, but Tempestrians tended to call him 'Michael' as they could never pronounce his real name correctly. Trust me, gentle reader, it is not as simple as it appears on the page. There were complex inflexions to be observed and several of the common mistakes apparently translated into something highly insulting in his language. So frankly, he'd rather they just stick to 'Michael.'

Standing at seven feet, with dried, translucent skin stretched like parchment over a horned skull, he was somewhat disconcerting to look at. Still, he was quite an amiable chap. Just as long as one did not mispronounce his name and he wasn't suffering from one of his bouts of depression, which were pretty understandable considering he was Fated to die at the end of every Final Battle. And there had been many Final Battles. Such death was not permanent – Daelen would always Resurrect him at a later time, but he could only do that when there was dire need.

On that fateful day, Michael was forced to leave Daelen's side, and try to defend the village, while the shadow warrior assailed Kullos with powerful blasts from his beam cannon and drew their great battle away from the area.

The being attacking the village, gentle reader, was difficult to see – a phrase I use quite literally. He certainly wasn't hiding, nor was it merely a case of camouflage. He wasn't invisible as such, but more like a 'void-creature.' When one looked at his position, one didn't really see him, so much as see the absence of him. As if there were a humanoid-shaped hole in the fabric of reality in the place he was standing. Michael had never seen anything like it before.

Or should that be, he had 'never not-seen nothing' like it before? Whatever. Let's just go with 'void-creature.'

Michael brought his powers to bear on this individual, but it remained unaffected. He summoned swarms of deadly insects, but they were swallowed by the void. He tried 'A Murder of Ravens in Fugue' bringing forth a dozen undead ravens from the Gates of Hell. Heralds of Death, they would inspire fear in those they attacked, but their calls seemed to echo and fade as if the void-creature were simply much too far away for their song to carry. Abandoning such tactics, he decided to go for a more direct approach, launching himself at the void-creature with his great Warhammer made of hardened, unbreakable petrified wood, which would imprison those it struck in the same material. The void-creature was fast – almost shadow warrior fast, but the centuries of training with Daelen paid off, and he finally hit his target. For a moment, the void-creature was cocooned, and it seemed the battle was won, but a moment later, the wood began to vibrate and quake until it shook itself apart, throwing Michael clear.

Michael rushed at the void-creature with his golden Sword of Maruk, imbued with the power of the gods, but the void-creature opened a pocket dimension, from which he produced a great cannon and aimed it at Michael. Time slowed as Michael looked on in horror: From his readings, it seemed like a version of what Daelen and Kullos used, only even more powerful.

Except it couldn't be.

The idea of a more powerful beam cannon was plausible enough in itself since the cannon drew power entirely from the shadow warrior who used it. In fact, the warrior was the real weapon – the cannon merely aided focus. A more powerful cannon really meant a more powerful shadow warrior. Just one problem: There were no more shadow warriors. Maybe not anywhere, but certainly in this realm, there were but three: Kullos, plus Daelen and his dark clone.

But if this attack was indeed what it appeared to be, then Michael could not survive. Michael could always sense when he was Fated to die, and this was not one of those occasions. The gods had created him with the knowledge that if ever he died when it wasn't Time, he could never be Resurrected. He would die, permanently. Forever.

In a last, desperate attempt to make his existence count for something, he channelled every last drop of power from his very being through his sword to strike at the void-creature. As he did so, three figures appeared between them. Again, Michael couldn't see them very well, but in a different way to the void-creature. They seemed to be

14

shrouded by magic. All he could make out through his haze of pain was that they seemed to have a more feminine silhouette, and each seemed to radiate a particular colour: one white, one black and one red. They had woven some kind of magical net between them, which had a lensing effect on both energy beams, magnifying Michael's and diffracting the cannon blast.

The result of this Intervention was threefold: First, Michael was thrown to the ground in agony, but still alive – barely. Second, the void-creature was stunned long enough for·the three newcomers to go on the offensive with what appeared to be a combination of all three flavours of mortal magic: wizard, cleric and druid. How mere mortal magic could be effective, Michael could not understand, but it was. The third effect of this Intervention, however, was that the portion of the diffracted cannon blast that had missed Michael slammed into the village around them. The young Catriona Redfletching was at the extreme edge of the explosion and was thrown clear. Others were not so fortunate. Cat dragged herself to her feet and cried out in tearful horror as her father, who had been only slightly closer to the blast, disintegrated into nothingness before her eyes.

Also witness to the horrific scene was Velena who had been hunting away from the village at the time of the attack. Cat sensed her mother before she saw her, and when she turned to look at her, she felt like her spirit had been ripped from her body. She knew well the look on her mother's face – it meant only one thing: the battle frenzy was upon her. Catriona's fears were confirmed as Velena dropped the carcass of the stag she had slain for their dinner and reached for her weapons.

"Mum! No!" Cat screamed, desperately, tears coursing like rivers down her cheeks. "You can't fight them, they're too powerful!"

But she could see it in her mother's eyes: at that moment, she didn't even recognise her own daughter. Catriona tried to physically stop her, but Velena threw her aside like she was nothing to her. That hurt Cat far more than the rock that struck her head as she landed on her back.

"Please!" she begged. "Please, Mum, I—I can't lose you, too!"

Velena ignored her pleas and rushed, heedless into battle, shooting arrows futilely at the void-creature.

"Mum," Cat whispered, her world fading as her concussion took its toll, and she lapsed into unconsciousness, "I…love…"

The three newcomers were holding the void-creature at bay with their combined magic but did not seem able to deal a decisive blow. Not until a fourth figure appeared, glowing with a light so bright, Michael wondered if a piece of the sun had somehow broken away and decided to shine in the night sky. Michael could not look at this creature of light directly, lest it damage his eyes. Through the delirium of pain, Michael thought he could detect a strange aura and a kind of magic that he couldn't identify.

The figure stood unflinching before the void-creature and said, "I can't allow you to interfere any further here. Go back to where you belong. You know I can make you, but I'm giving you this one chance to leave by your own power."

The void-creature spoke for the first time. Michael suspected it would have been terrifying even without the heavy distortion that surrounded it, but he was in too much pain to give it any real thought.

"If I go," it said, "I'll not be doing you any favours. It would be easier on all of you if I succeeded this day. Back home, your tricks won't work on me the way they do here. You know that."

"Yes, I know," the other admitted, "but that is how it must be."

"Fine, we'll do it your way. See you later!"

With that, the void-creature opened a portal and stepped through it.

Once the void-creature was gone, Michael observed the four newcomers quickly consult one another over something. Apparently, an agreement was reached because the first three faded from reality, leaving just the last one behind alone. The glowing figure continued to defy any analysis, remaining incorporeal and insubstantial as it floated towards Michael.

"Greetings, Ossian Miach Kaidool," came an ethereal voice. To Michael's astonishment, they pronounced his name perfectly.

Michael always described the sound as 'barely more than a whisper,' and yet with 'a kind of hidden musical quality' that he couldn't really explain.

"I can help you," said the figure, "but I will only do so on one condition: as a demigod, I know you have perception beyond that of mortals and a direct line to the gods. I am about to have an important meeting with someone, and neither you nor the gods must know anything about it. The pain you're suffering right now is blocking all that out, so leaving you as you are would serve my needs perfectly. But I'm not without compassion, so I'm willing to take your pain away, if you agree to my taking away all your other senses, too." The figure paused for a moment and appeared to reconsider. "Actually, I can leave you your sight, because nothing you see will matter without the wider context. Don't worry, it will only be for a short while. Daelen's latest fight with Kullos will soon be over, and he'll come back here to help you, but I must be gone before he arrives, so I need your answer now. Do you consent to my terms?"

"Yes," Michael gasped. "The pain...is too...too much, I...I consent."

The instant the words left his mouth, all of his higher senses vanished, taking the pain with it. He couldn't feel anything at all or hear, or taste, or smell. The stranger was true to their word, however, and left him with his sight intact. Michael almost wished he had asked them to take that away, too, given the terrible carnage and devastation all around. But since he felt at least partially responsible for it, Michael accepted that he had no right to be shielded from it, so he looked on.

The figure seemed to crouch down beside the still form of Catriona Redfletching and gently wake her with a touch. Cat stirred and opened her eyes. She looked puzzled for a moment as if she couldn't quite work out what she was doing there. Then the memory rushed back, and the half-Faery girl shot to her feet, darting away as if trying to find something or someone. The ethereal figure seemed torn between trying to comfort or help Catriona, and impatiently checking what Michael assumed to be a timepiece on their wrist. As if some pressing need were threatening to drag them away against their wishes. After a short while, Cat sank to the ground once more, in the middle of the devastation that had been her home but moments before and buried her head in her hands. That was the moment the shrouded figure chose to approach her once more.

Michael was unable to hear the words that were said, but he guessed they must have been profound indeed, for they were enough for the distraught Catriona to look up and cease her tears. The girl seemed fascinated by the other's presence as if they presented a puzzle intriguing enough to put her grief aside for the moment. Cat gazed at the other like she could not believe they were even real but couldn't fathom why she felt that way.

After a short conversation, the shrouded figure convinced Catriona to stand and watch as the mage opened a pocket dimension and produced a small wooden staff, approximately three feet in height with a large blue crystal on top. Then the figure performed magic on the land, causing the grass to regrow, trees to mend and flowers to bloom. In short order, the village and its buildings were restored, not quite to their original design, but a fair approximation of it, as if they were reconstructing it not from recent memory, but from something more distant. The mage's talents did not extend to bringing back the people who were lost that day, but by the time they were finished, at least those Quarthonian survivors that remained had somewhere to rebuild their lives. All through this, the crystal at the head of the staff sent a lightshow high into the sky, but frankly, Cat was far more interested in what was happening to the land.

Catriona looked on with wide-eyed astonishment, while all the other mortals seemed baffled by this apparent miracle. Some of them lifted their heads in praise to their gods, though Michael knew they had nothing to do with it. Others fell to their knees to worship Tempestria itself, perhaps in reverence to Blessed Alycia, Mother of Nature. Somehow, Michael thought this was nearer the mark, but none of them seemed to link what was happening with the mysterious figure floating beside Catriona. It was as if they could not perceive them at all. None except Michael and of course the young Catriona.

When the magical demonstration was done, the figure gave the staff to Catriona, who beheld it in wonder. The mage began to move away as if they were going to use the distraction of their gift to make good their escape, but then, as if pulled by unseen forces of compassion, they swooped back over to Catriona and embraced her. When they broke the hug, the mysterious figure took one more glance at their timepiece. It seemed that their time was finally up, for they stepped away from Catriona and began to fade. As they did so, Michael's senses came flooding back, along with the agonising pain.

"I'm sorry, my friend," came the whispered, melodic voice in his mind. "I think I might have forgotten to mention this part of our agreement. Sorry." And then they were gone.

*****

18

My mother always referred to that glowing figure as her 'Angel,' but to this day, even with all our abilities, the Angel's shroud remains impenetrable to all our scans. I only know what happened through a much later telepathic link with Michael, seeing his memory of events. Our best guess is that they were a future Guardian. Assuming we still have a future by the time I'm finished.

Investigation through Interactive Time travel is entirely out of the question. It's a Temporal Black Spot where all are forbidden to venture, employing magical wards to prevent entry, and I know better than to try to breach them.

To interfere too often with the same events is potentially catastrophic. Time Intervention is not something the Guardians take lightly. Apart from myself, they are the only ones with the necessary knowledge and skill. Anyone else would be destroyed and scattered in the void like a dandelion in a hurricane.

Yes, I know I'm in the middle of an Illegal Time Intervention at this very moment (relatively speaking), but I assure you I would never endanger reality simply to satisfy my selfish curiosity about my mother's Angel! Besides, this was the worst day of my mother's life; Michael's memory of watching an innocent young girl have her whole world ripped apart was distressing enough. I have no desire to witness it first-hand. I don't know how she bore it. I'm certain I could not.

It took time to find out exactly what happened to Velena. In all the terror and confusion, keeping track of one individual had been difficult. But there were enough eyewitness accounts to confirm that she, like many others, was simply vaporised.

In later life, whenever Catriona spoke of these events, she always described her mother fighting with a ferocity that rivalled the void storms in the sky. She chose to remember Velena desperately giving her life to save the daughter she loved. While that may not match the account that I have written, gentle reader, I'm sure you can understand why my mother would prefer her own memory of events.

But I promised you that every word of this story would be true, so I shall not sugar coat these events…or those yet to come.

Chapter 3

It was a few years later, and Catriona Redfletching was talking to an old White wizard named Renjaf.

"Oh, come on!" she pleaded, "It's not like I'm asking for the moon!"

Renjaf was something of a recluse. He lived in a tall tower, as was the fashion for wizards in those days, that sat within several acres of much-neglected land a few miles from the town of Compton, leaving only rarely. Why was Catriona there, gentle reader? The answer to that requires some explanation.

It naturally took some time for Cat to come to terms with everything that had happened, but eventually, life went on, as it always does. Pyrah helped enormously, with her frequent visits.

Who is Pyrah?

Well, not all higher planar beings appear human. They may manifest in all manner of guises. Pyrah, gentle reader, was one such creature, who seemed to be a small, green, highly venomous snake that had been Catriona's friend and protector since she was a child. Cat first met her while playing in the forest around her father's Quarthonian home. Pyrah had been injured, caught in the middle of another of Daelen's battles. That time it was not against Kullos, but rather his dark clone, although that was a distinction without difference when dodging beam cannon blasts.

Cat said, "hello," and was astonished when the snake said '*hello*' back.

Well, not 'said' exactly, but communicated certainly – communicated sympathically. Let me see…how to explain sympathic communication… More than empathy, less than telepathy. Not that you can draw a straight line through the three. Sympathic communication involves the transmission of concepts. So rather than saying, "I am your friend," Pyrah simply transmitted the concept, the idea of friendship. It didn't allow for much in the way of subtlety in those days, but thanks to Catriona's efforts to nurse her back to health, they managed to develop a powerful bond. Pyrah was sorry she had not been around to help when Cat lost her parents. Catriona was glad she had been absent. Otherwise, she might have lost her, too.

Still, there was no denying things had changed for Catriona. Before the day she lost her parents, the Day of the Monster, the Day of the Angel, Cat had been a promising student at magic school – a relatively new concept at the time, but one that would eventually supplant the old apprentice system. Three years later, her grades at college were mediocre at best. It just didn't hold her interest as it had before. Now, she was more interested in her Angel.

I should point out that my mother didn't really consider her miraculous visitor to have been an Angel in the literal sense. It was just that she couldn't think of another label she could use that fitted any better. She dearly wished for something better, though, for one reason above all others: everybody said her Angel wasn't real.

To everybody else who was there that day, the restoration of their village was an unexplained miracle, and they seemed happy for it to remain so. Not Catriona. Everybody attributed her imaginary guardian Angel to an expression of her grief. A way of dealing with the trauma and even survivor guilt. Her way of explaining the inexplicable, why she survived when others only a few feet away from her – her father included – did not.

'Poor Catriona' people would say. 'It must be so hard for her to accept that there was no reason, just random chance.'

'Give her time,' the experts said. 'In time, she will see and learn to accept it.'

But she never did.

She knew her Angel was real. How else did she acquire her 'Crystal Mage Staff' as she had named her gift, mostly for the convenience of having *something* to call it. She didn't want to give it some grandiose name like 'The Great Staff of Zarathon' or 'The Mystical Rod of Destiny' or 'The Almighty Staff of the Gods.' No. It was a simple wooden staff, something that mages liked to use to channel magic and it had a large blue crystal on the top. Hence 'Crystal Mage Staff.' Simple. Unassuming. Unpretentious. Although, it did radiate a kind of higher planar energy that Cat did not understand, buried beneath layers upon layers of security and protection.

Her Angel had warned her not to tamper with that energy, "Except," they said, "in the event of some dire emergency of worldwide, cataclysmic proportions. And even then, think twice."

Catriona kept that part to herself. No sense in drawing attention to it if it were that important. There were always those who were covetous of power and might seek to take the staff from her. She could never allow that. She herself was hardly likely to be involved in any 'dire emergency of worldwide, cataclysmic proportions.' Besides, she wasn't interested in power as such. She was much more interested in acquiring knowledge. Specifically, knowledge relating to the Crystal Mage Staff, because that was her only link to her Angel.

On a more practical level, her Angel had inspired her to look at druid magic in a new way. Of the three principal flavours of magic, druid abilities were something of a poor cousin next to wizardry and clerical magic.

Not knowing how magic works on your world, gentle reader, or indeed whether any such equivalent exists where you are, I should break off for a moment to explain how it works on Tempestria. To put that in its proper context, however, I first need to discuss dimensional cosmology.

*****

Although I've been alive for a thousand years or so, I look like a human girl of about twenty, and perhaps it's vain of me, but I like to try and stay in touch with people who really are that young. One of the best ways to do that, I have found, is to go back to college and be a student again for a while. After all, a lot has changed in the last millennium, so there's always more to learn.

So, to help me explain things to you now, I'm going to borrow from one of my many college dissertations:

THE GREAT COSMIC SANDWICH

Barring some grand, cosmic catastrophe, all mortal worlds exist in the middle of The Great Cosmic Sandwich.

The layer above is the cheese, aka the realm of the gods. There are a wide variety of gods to choose from, different gods suit different people according to their tastes, and quite frankly, some of them stink. The layer immediately below is the first of the demonic planes – I like to think of them as the tomato layer with all that red simulating blood. No-one knows precisely how many layers there are below that, although I'm convinced one of them must be pickles. Apologies to anyone who likes them – it's all a matter of taste of course, but to me, they are vile

22

and disgusting things and surely sent from hell itself. Besides, some people like to 'pickle' specimens in jars for all manner of strange experiments. This fits symbolically with what those Greater Demons tend to do with the unfortunate mortals they snatch when they make their way up through the planes of reality to the mortal realm.

Above the gods, there are other creatures, mostly beyond mortal comprehension. To me, these are the sauces: adding to the overall flavour of the cosmos without contributing anything of nutritional value and – if your sandwich shops are anything like ours, gentle reader – not always what you expected to get when you ordered. Similarly, with rare exceptions, these higher planar beings contribute little of substance to the cosmos, from a mortal's point of view, but neither do they do any harm. Then you have the shadow realm where my father and his people come from – more on them later. For now, suffice to say they are the lettuce in the sandwich. They're good for us, and they know it. In fact, they're so good for us, they're going to help us whether we like it or not. The trouble is, since they are so good for us, they're convinced they're better than mortals. Frankly, I'm rather more interested in the meaty bit in the middle – that's mortals along with the Guardians and, if I may be so bold, myself – although if I'm honest, a good, well-balanced sandwich is probably best for all of us.

Of course, all the fillings of the Great Cosmic Sandwich need something to contain them. At the bottom, the deepest part of the demonic planes is home to the Keeper of the Underworld, often seen as some kind of Source of Evil, topped by a spread of fallen Angels. But I can't help thinking that I, too, would probably be a bit grumpy, if I were always being squished by the weight of the universe pressing down on me like I was a flattened slice of bread. At the other end, at the pinnacle of the sandwich, the crowning glory, as it were, the Creator stands on the shoulders of their own spread of Angels, who think they're the best thing next to sliced bread. As for the Creator themselves, I see them as a large bun: risen too high, over-inflated with their own self-importance and probably slightly burnt on top.

I should probably point out, gentle reader, that my college dissertation was, in point of fact, marked down for my 'flippant treatment of the subject matter.' But this is my story, my world that's in danger and as my mother's Angel put it, this is indeed a 'dire emergency of worldwide cataclysmic proportions,' so I'll be as flippant as I like.

Oh, and in case you think my mother's staff is somehow the key to my saving the world, gentle reader, you're absolutely right. It doesn't have any power anymore, the last of it faded centuries ago, but it is the perfect device for wedging my bedroom door shut so that the Red and Black Guardians can't get out. Physics of triangles plus an adaptive anti-magic field and two of the world's most powerful individuals have to take it in turns to take a nap on my bed. Well, I suppose they could squeeze up and share, but I don't think they're that close! Is that flippant enough for you?

Actually, all flippancy aside, in complete and utter seriousness, there is a compulsory side order to our Sandwich. A force, an entity infinitely more dangerous than the Keeper of the Underworld. *IT* is formless, *IT* is genderless. *IT* is the enemy of life and structure and Creation itself. *IT* is the antithesis of order but calling *IT* chaos is to try to put *IT* in a box that is far too small to contain *ITs* nature. *IT* is nameless; the only term we have for this entity is '*IT*.' *IT* cannot be killed or destroyed, for death and destruction are *ITs* food and drink.

The Guardians and I stand against *IT* and must be constantly vigilant against *IT*, especially when we Intervene in Time. If we get things wrong, we could unravel Time and the whole of Creation. That's why the current Black and Red Guardians are so against what Mandalee and I are doing: they're afraid and justifiably so. I'm not going to sit here and say we have no choice, because we do. Our choice is to act, fully aware of the risk. That's why I'm writing this.

I'm sure you're wondering what danger we could possibly be facing that we would risk everything to do this, but I can't tell you yet. Sure, I could give you a name – unlike *IT*, this threat does have one – but I might as well call him 'Bob' for all that it would mean to you. What you need is context, and that takes time.

Fortunately, gentle reader, I'm something of an expert in that field.

Chapter 4

Now, where was I before I got carried away by the Great Cosmic Sandwich? Ah yes, magic.

Clerical magic came first, historically speaking. The gods feed on the worship of mortals and to help encourage this, it was in their interests to use some of their powers to help mortals achieve things down here. It made mortals more inclined to worship them if they felt they were getting something from it. Clerics grew powerful in this way, but there was a drawback: gods are often fickle and determining what might please them from one moment to the next was challenging, to say the least. That made their magic unreliable at times.

Some people got fed up with this dance with the gods and postulated that mortals could achieve the same results by themselves with patience and study. They believed that the clerics' real source of power was not the gods themselves, but a power that the gods refined from the inter-planar repulsion forces. Simply put, that which allowed the planes of reality to remain separate and distinct. Over time, wizards learned to take this power for themselves, and their spells grew to match clerical prayers in power and intensity.

There was a third group known as druids, who were worried about draining inter-planar forces by either gods or mortals. However vast and immeasurable these forces might be, they were surely finite. What if those forces were weakened as a result? What if that caused the planes of reality to touch in ways they were never meant to? What if it was happening already? What if that was why their world was constantly assailed by demons? What if the growing use of inter-planar repulsion forces as magic was bringing the demon realms somehow closer, thereby making it easier for them to sort of jump or climb up or whatever it was demons did to get here?

Druids didn't use those forces for their magic. Instead, they used the 'Providence of Blessed Alycia, Mother of Nature' – the ancient name for the kind of subtle energy that emanated from Tempestria itself. This kind of energy, they believed, actually healed the cosmos, replenishing that which wizards and clerics took for themselves. The drawback: it simply wasn't as powerful, and so it never caught on except in the areas of healing and garden maintenance. Most druids did not seek to stop the other two flavours being used. They simply sought a state of balance where their magic could effectively recycle that which the others used. Unfortunately, no-one had found a way to make druid magic work in a way that could even remotely achieve this. In fact, it was generally believed to be impossible.

Catriona knew better. She had seen it. What her Angel did on that fateful day was unlike anything wizards or clerics could achieve. Others might think it was an inexplicable miracle, but to her, the explanation was simple: druid magic, and she wanted to learn how it was done. It became her personal quest, for which her only lead was the staff. It didn't matter if others told her it was an 'unhealthy obsession borne out of grief and loss.' It didn't matter if nobody else thought her Angel was real. Catriona knew better.

What hurt the most was the pity she would see on the faces of people she knew. Sympathy for the 'poor young woman' who had lost everything…including her mind. Still, she would not be swayed from her chosen course. It was her life, and if her parents had taught her anything, it was that she was damn well going to live it her way.

There was, of course, one other individual who Cat knew could most likely back up her 'version of events' as people liked to call it: Michael. Needless to say, though, he didn't get out much, and he was currently unavailable, on account of having died in Daelen's latest Final Battle against Kullos. Which she felt was as inconvenient for her as she supposed it was for him to be stuck in his Deepest Slumber. It wasn't as if she could roll up to the front door of his tomb and knock very loudly until he woke up. For one thing, Daelen StormTiger had set up defences that, given the shadow warrior's power, she could not hope to counter. Besides, regardless of anything she might do, Michael would Sleep until the Time of Greatest Need and clearly, helping Catriona Redfletching did not count. Which once again left her with her staff.

She began to research both its security and its history – something that took her time away from what her college tutors kept telling her she ought to be studying. She often wondered how they could possibly believe they knew better than her what she 'ought' to be studying.

*****

One day, her class had a visitor in the form of the head of the Black robe mages, Laethyn. He was there to talk about the history of wizard magic. In days gone by, Cat conceded she would have been interested. Now all she felt was irritation. Where was the talk on the history of druid magic? Even when Laethyn waved the famous *Nameless Book* in the air, Catriona barely raised an eyebrow.

The *Nameless Book*, gentle reader, was neither nameless nor a book.

OK, in the most basic sense, it *was* a book, but in another way – given the layers upon layers of magical protection that prevented it from being opened – it was the most heavily fortified installation of magic ever constructed. As for the title, it was only Nameless in the sense that nobody knew what it was called, because it was written in a completely unknown language. According to legend, the book had been the work of Magias, the first wizard, based on the evidence of dating techniques applied to the book itself. It was the closest thing that secular wizard society had to a sacred religious artefact. According to tradition, Laethyn would keep possession of the *Nameless Book* until he retired, at which time he would pass it on to either the Red or White leader, depending on which of them had seniority.

Catriona was sitting too far away to make any significant observations beyond a mild surprise that a book that was supposedly almost a thousand years old should be in such good condition. Still, modern magic had developed remarkable preservation techniques, so it was no great mystery. The students, in general, were not allowed to touch the precious object or even get close. As if breathing on it might somehow cause damage to something that was unmarked by the passage of centuries.

Despite her general disinterest, though, the college did have resources that my mother thought might be useful to her, so she continued to attend and do just enough to keep from being removed from classes entirely.

Information on her staff was extremely hard to come by. Cat chased many a wild goose down many a dead end, but little by little she found references to help her. Through a combination of obscure books, tenacious research and experimentation, her druid magic began to grow, and she unlocked the first layer of her staff's protection.

One of her favourite things she learned, gentle reader, was shapeshifting magic. It involved the careful manipulation of her body and what we would these days call her genetic structure, although that knowledge was unknown at that time in my mother's life, and I'm sure

27

she never thought about it in those terms. Mostly, druid magic works on knowledge, instinct and a strong belief that you can do what you are trying to do. Almost as if one is talking to Blessed Alycia herself and explaining what you're trying to achieve, and no matter how clumsy one's explanation might be, if you have the right attitude, she seems to smile upon the druid, and it happens. As knowledge and understanding grow, however, the magic becomes easier and more controlled.

Catriona's favourite form quickly became that of a red-banded falcon, so named for the pair of red stripes that encircled its legs. Now, there is no such thing as a red-banded falcon, but the red bands helped to serve as an anchor to her true self, linking in her mind with her name and of course her mother's: Redfletching. Flying was undeniably a fast and convenient way to travel, but the problem she had was how to carry her staff around with her. There was no way she would leave it anywhere – it never left her side. Here, her decision to keep her foot in the door at wizarding college paid dividends as she became interested in a course on Advanced Dimensional Harmonics.

These days, gentle reader, what she learned would be considered *Basic Misconceptions* in Dimensional Harmonics, but that's progress for you! Still, through creative combinations of this course material with her own independent study and druid magic, she found a way to put her staff, her clothes and anything else her half-Faery self might need in a kind of pocket dimension, such that it was always effectively right next to her, within reach, no matter where she was. It was crude, it was tiring, and it was unstable, causing her belongings to fall out of her pocket dimension at inconvenient times…or even fall *in*, sometimes leading to her find herself suddenly naked with her backpack on her head.

OK, I'm being flippant again, but I certainly don't mean to mock. All the techniques we take for granted today had to start somewhere, and my mother was a pioneer in this field…just sometimes a *naked* pioneer. But I digress.

By now, gentle reader, you must be wondering what all this has to do with Catriona's conversation with that old White wizard recluse. Well, as I have said, my mother was obsessed with researching her Crystal Mage Staff. She would pursue tenaciously any strand of a clue, and one such strand led her to believe that the wizard Renjaf had in his possession, a particular book that other references had hinted contained such information. Yes, I know that's a bit tentative, but it was good enough for my mother, so she went to see him.

The problem with this idea lies in the word 'recluse.'

Renjaf was one of those people who simply didn't have much use for other people and would prefer to be left alone. He was a grumpy old man with poor eyesight and terrible manners.

*****

The door was yanked open, suddenly.

"Who are you?" a scowling, squinting Renjaf snarled before Cat could get a word in. "You don't look like my usual delivery boy!"

"Oh, no," she giggled. "I'm sure I don't! In fact, I'm quite glad I don't look like him. Not that there's anything wrong with how he looks, as far as I know. I just don't really want to look like a boy at all." She giggled again. "And I'm afraid I don't have any delivery to give you. In fact, I want to get something from you. I—"

He slammed the door in her face. She knocked again and the door opened.

"Sorry, bit nervous," she said. "Short version: all I want is a book."

"A book?"

"Yes," she confirmed. "Specifically, something called *Shifting Stars*; it's pretty rare from what I gather. In fact, you have the only copy as far as I can tell. You see, I have this staff," she held it up to show him.

He tried to slam the door again, but Cat was quicker and shoved her staff in the door.

"Please, let just let me pop in and borrow the book and I'll be out of your hair. I've been working on a locator spell that should be able to find a specific title pretty quickly. Or you can get the book, if that's easier – although, given your eyesight, I'm not sure it would be, no offence. Can you still read, these days? Either way, your hair will be free of me."

"Go away!" he yelled.

"Not until I get that book," Cat insisted. "Sorry, but it's really important to me. Look, I'll pay you for it," she offered.

"Don't want your money."

"Alright then, I'll trade you for it! Anything you want. Name it, and I'll get it for you."

"Don't want anything from you! I just want you gone!"

"Oh, come on!" Catriona pleaded. "It's not like I'm asking for the moon! Actually, I'll give you the moon if that's what you want. I mean, I'm not exactly sure how I'd do it, but that's not the point. The point is I'm willing to give you the moon if you'll just give me what I want. A moon for a book – that's not a bad deal! Please just let me have it."

By the way, gentle reader, if you were wondering where I get my tendency to ramble, I trust that question has now been answered to your satisfaction.

Forcing herself to calm down, Catriona asked, simply, "Why not? Just tell me that. What would it cost you just to let me borrow one book?"

"Nothing," Renjaf said. "Just don't care."

"What do you mean?"

"I mean I don't and never ever will care! My whole life nobody ever did a damn thing for me, so why should I do anything for anybody else?"

Cat was so stunned by that response that she involuntarily stepped back and relaxed her grip on her staff. The wizard kicked it out of her grasp, and it skittered down the path, forcing her to scamper after it. Renjaf waited until she retrieved it and ran back, and then deliberately slammed the door in her face. Cat yelped in pain, her eyes watering. Just a bit more force and he could easily have broken her nose. In fact, she wasn't altogether sure he hadn't been trying.

Still, she refused to get angry.

"I'm sorry you feel that way, Mr Renjaf," Cat said to the closed door, "but one way or another I'm getting that book. Tell you what: I *will* do something for you! I'll…I don't know…" she paused to consider.

As she looked around for inspiration, she could see how the grounds were grown wild and out of control. It seemed to Cat that it wouldn't be long before Renjaf's delivery boy would have to bring an axe to cut his way through a forest just to reach the door.

"I'll work on your garden!" she declared, triumphantly. "I'm a druid – druid magic is great for garden maintenance!"

Still no response.

She had no idea if he could still hear her, but it didn't matter – even with his bad eyesight, he'd be able to see the results soon enough.

And so, Catriona spent all of her free time for the next few days, tidying and reshaping the land, gathering up fallen leaves and branches, removing the moss from paths, cleaning up the overgrown pond she had discovered, and encouraging flowers to grow.

Then, one day, as she was regrowing the wooden fence that surrounded the property, the delivery boy turned up with a horse and cart decked out in a distinctive blue and white company livery. The gate wasn't wide enough for his transport, so he dismounted. The boy began to struggle up the long path on foot, armed with a load of heavy groceries and Catriona saw an opportunity.

Chapter 5

As I gaze through Time, gentle reader, I can watch my mother living her life. I've done that for a long, long time. Ever since I first discovered that I could manipulate the temporal dimensions in this way. Given this ability, you might expect me to watch the major events for which she is renowned: her roles in the Fall of Kullos, establishing the Guardianship, battling demons, defeating an Angel. But often, I get the greatest joy from her, shall we say, less than stellar moments. They make me feel better about my own mistakes, mishaps and misunderstandings. Perhaps my favourite of these is the story of 'The Cat Who Smelled of Horse.'

*****

Catriona immediately rushed over to give the delivery boy a helping hand.

"Hi," she said, "I'd shake your hand, but you don't seem to have one free. If I can take some of that stuff for you, then you will."

"Oh, thanks a lot, miss…?" he replied, handing out some of the bags.

"I'm Catriona," she said, shaking his now free hand, "but you can call me Cat because we're friends now."

"Jacob," he said, returning the handshake, "and that's Bonnie," he added, indicating his horse. "So, Cat, what brings you out here? I've never seen anybody visit old Renjaf before. Are you a relative?"

"Oh no," she said. "I'm just helping out, you know, tidying up the grounds and making sure your deliveries get through."

Jacob looked around in amazement. "Is all this you?"

She nodded. "Yep, all me. Been busy."

"I can see that. Well, you've certainly made my job easier, so thanks for that."

"No problem, it's a public service."

"I'm sure the old guy will appreciate it."

"You'd think so, wouldn't you?" Cat agreed. "So, if I were to ask him for one teeny, tiny little thing in return, like, say, I don't know, just for instance, a book. That would be perfectly reasonable, right?"

"A book?"

"I'll explain later," she said. "For now, let's just deliver these groceries!"

She gave him an enthusiastic punch on the shoulder and regretted it instantly when he looked at her strangely.

They had reached the door by now and, trying to cover her embarrassment, she cleared her throat and asked, "Do you want to knock or shall I?"

Jacob did it himself.

"How does this work?" Cat asked. "We go inside and drop all this off in his kitchen, or something?"

Jacob laughed, "No, I leave it just inside the door."

That wasn't as good as Cat had hoped, but still, it was *inside* the tower, which was closer than she had been so far.

When the moment came, however, the wizard only let Jacob inside, using his magic to keep Catriona on the doorstep while snatching the bags from her hand.

Doing her best to seize the moment, she said, "Jacob here was just saying he thought I'd done a good job with your grounds, Mr Renjaf, and he thought it would be pretty reasonable if you were to give me that book I wanted, in return."

"Well, I didn't exactly—" Jacob began, but Cat shushed him to cut him off.

"So, what do you say? Deal?"

Renjaf's response, gentle reader, was something rude and offensive that I see no need to write here. Suffice to say, as Jacob stepped back outside and began to head back down the path, Catriona was left once again staring at the door, frustrated, hands on hips.

Not one to give up, though, a new approach formulated in her mind. After all, there was clearly at least one person who was allowed inside Renjaf's door. If she could just get where Jacob had been a moment ago, she would need only a moment longer to get what she wanted.

"So, Mr Renjaf," she muttered to herself, quietly, "I don't look like your usual delivery boy, eh? Well, I'll just have to see what I can do about that."

Calling out to the delivery boy, she asked, "Jacob, where are you off to now?"

"Back to Compton," he replied.

"Great! Any chance of a lift?"

"Sure," he shrugged. "No problem."

"Excellent, thanks," she said, linking arms with Jacob as they walked back down the path. Jacob seemed surprised but didn't object. "So, tell me about yourself: do you come this way often…"

During the ride back to the town, Catriona flirted shamelessly with Jacob, learning everything she needed to know to pull off her plan. Studying his face, his body, his voice, committing it all to memory. She found out that Renjaf's deliveries mostly ran to a specific schedule, and so Jacob would be out that way again in just a few days. Catriona got him to agree to her joining him, on the pretext of her doing more work on the grounds in hopes of gaining Renjaf's favour. Of course, she didn't really need any help getting out there, her falcon form being much quicker than any horse, but he didn't need to know that. That's how Catriona got there over the next few days, to work on the grounds some more. She brought Renjaf bottles of wine, chocolates, pastries from the bakery, anything she could think of to persuade him to change his mind, but nothing moved him, so her plan went ahead.

*****

When the day rolled around, to make things as easy as possible, she had decided to forgo her customary red wizard's robes for a simple top and trousers.

This time there wasn't as much to carry, so Cat made sure she grabbed everything almost before the horse had stopped. Jacob called for her to wait up, but she only walked faster. Once inside the grounds of the wizard's tower, she used her magic to cause a few of the plants to reach out and grab Jacob so he couldn't move. She even persuaded them to place a broadleaf over his mouth so he couldn't cry out.

Once she judged herself sufficiently far away, she concentrated hard and shapeshifted her body to match the image of Jacob that she had in her mind. When she looked at her reflection in the pond, she was reasonably satisfied.

"Not bad," she said, in a slightly deeper voice than usual. It wasn't perfect, but it should be good enough to fool someone from a distance or someone with poor eyesight.

Steeling herself, she walked the remaining distance to Renjaf's door and knocked.

Cat had her locator spell fully prepared in her mind, ready to cast the instant she was inside, then she could run after it, find the book, pop it in her pocket dimension and get out again before the old wizard knew what had happened or that she'd taken anything.

After a moment, the door opened.

"Good morning, Mr Renjaf," said Catriona, brightly, in Jacob's voice. "I've got your delivery for you if you'll just let me pop in with it, OK?"

Renjaf scowled and squinted at 'Jacob.'

"Something different about you," he growled.

"Who m-me?" she stammered. "N-no, I don't think so…"

She had to stifle a giggle. It was something she did when she was nervous, but it wasn't really 'in character' for Jacob.

"Oh!" 'Jacob' cried in sudden inspiration. "New haircut."

Catriona's real self had long ginger hair halfway down her back – she'd been growing it out since she was little – whereas Jacob's hair was dark and short. She did worry that she'd made it a bit *too* short, though, when shapeshifting in a hurry. She also hoped she would remember how long her own hair should be when she changed back.

Of course, gentle reader, my mother could have used her magic to grow her hair as long as she wished, but she always considered that cheating, somehow.

So far, her real self had always snapped back on cue, but she supposed there was a chance that it wouldn't. That's why she still added a pair of small red bands when she shifted, as an anchor to her real self. They were currently around 'Jacob's' left ankle where they were covered by 'his' socks so they wouldn't be conspicuous.

With another grunt, Renjaf, apparently satisfied, stepped aside, and finally Catriona found herself inside his home. She wasted not a moment looking around before placing the bags on the floor and casting her locator spell, which the druidess followed with her mind as it shot up the stairs to Renjaf's library on the tenth floor. In seconds, she would have a precise location, but her attention wavered as she felt something brushing against her back. Something familiar and yet somehow wrong: her hair.

"Uh-oh!" she cried.

While casting her locator spell, she had inadvertently let go of her image of Jacob and reverted to her old self.

"You!" Renjaf cried, his face darkening like the sky preparing for a thunderstorm. "Get out of my house!"

"Look, I'm sorry, OK?" Cat said, holding up her arms in surrender.

Damn, she had been so close!

"I just really need that book. That's all! Really! There's no need to—" but she never got to finish her sentence as Renjaf picked her up with his magic and literally threw her out of his home, through the air and into the pond where she landed with a splash.

After crawling her way out of the water, she stood up and walked back down the path, where she freed Jacob. He was understandably livid.

"What the hell was that?" he demanded.

"The plants wouldn't have harmed you," Cat assured him. "I just needed you out of the way."

Jacob shook his head, "You don't get it, do you? I wasn't worried about the plants."

"Then what?" Cat wondered with a puzzled frown.

"It's pretty solitary, this job of mine," he said. "Not much chance to meet people. I know Renjaf's a grumpy old miser, but even the polite customers aren't interested in getting to know the delivery boy. Still, here I thought I'd actually made a friend. But no! You were just using me, weren't you?"

A dripping wet Cat reluctantly nodded. "Yes, I was," she admitted, quietly. "I hadn't thought of it like that, but you're right. I'm sorry."

"At least you're honest about it," Jacob allowed.

"Oh yes, I'm fully prepared to be completely honest about my total dishonesty," she quipped.

Despite himself, Jacob laughed, "You know you could have just asked me to help, right?"

"It never occurred to me," she confessed. "When it comes to this staff of mine, well, everybody thinks my story is insane, so I tend to keep it to myself." There was a pause for a moment, then she said, "So, what now?"

"Well, I've got more deliveries to do around Compton..."

"Alright."

"...and after what you pulled today, I should just leave you here."

"Absolutely fair enough. You should probably do that."

36

"But I'm not going to."

"You're not?"

"Come on," he said, taking her arm, "Let's see what we can do about getting you dry."

"Only if you're sure," Cat said.

"Well, I can't leave a half-drowned Cat to fend for herself, now can I?" Jacob quipped, taking her arm and leading her back to his cart.

"Well, OK, then," Cat smiled. "If you put it like that, thanks. I just don't want to be any trouble."

Jacob snorted, "You've already been that, and you really shouldn't thank me yet – there is a price: On the way, you can tell me your 'insane' story, so I know exactly who it is I've made friends with."

"That's fair," Cat agreed.

"Also," Jacob added, "the only blankets I have are for Bonnie, so before long you're going to smell like a horse."

"'The Cat Who Smelled of Horse'!" Catriona laughed. "They'll be telling the story a thousand years from now."

*****

And so, gentle reader, here I am, doing exactly that!

One of the reasons I include this part of my mother's story is to provide balance. Catriona Redfletching is a legend, but she was once a person, and like all of us, she was flawed, fallible. She made mistakes.

I just hope, for all our sakes, that I am not making one now.

Chapter 6

It occurs to me to point out, gentle reader, that my mother wasn't *completely* obsessed with her quest for knowledge of her staff, her Angel and her magic. She was, for the most part, a well-rounded young woman with an active social life. She still had a few friends and relationships with both Faery and humans, though she was never particularly close to any of them. She had learned not to discuss her Angel for fear of accusations of insanity, or her staff for fear of drawing too much attention to it. Even her advancing druid magic was seen as little more than a curiosity, like an obscure hobby that nobody else gets unless they share it.

Except nobody did.

Jacob was different. When Catriona opened up to him, he did not judge her sanity. If she said she saw a sort-of-Angel who gave her the staff and mended her village with druid magic, then Jacob was prepared to accept it. After all, as Cat herself argued, she had clearly got her staff from somewhere – it could hardly have just been lying around, unnoticed for who knows how long.

As for the 'miraculous' restoration of her home, he said, "I don't believe miracles really happen."

"Miracles can happen if people make them happen," Catriona countered.

Still, from what Jacob had seen Catriona do with druid magic – tending Renjaf's grounds and getting the plants to restrain him – it didn't seem an unreasonable extrapolation. He was only sorry that the stubborn old goat in his tower was standing in the way of something so crucial to Cat when co-operating would cost him next to nothing. He promised to help her in any way he could, but for now, Catriona had no further ideas of how she was going to get her hands on that book.

There did not seem to be any other copies of the book. From what Catriona could gather, it had never been what one could call popular, being considered a fringe text at best, and the ravings of a madman at worst. However, given how quick people were to question her own sanity, she wasn't willing to dismiss the anonymous author of *Shifting Stars* so easily.

*****

Catriona's friendship with Jacob grew strong over the following weeks and months, even to the point of moving in together. Although it was never a romantic relationship as such, she was always quite happy to get physical with the right person under the right circumstances. Indeed, there were a few more incidents of her pocket dimension swallowing their clothes, which led them to take full advantage.

Everyday life continued for the best part of a year until Cat came home from college mid-afternoon, one day, and was surprised to find Jacob there.

"What are you doing home?" she asked. "You were going all the way out to old Renjaf's place, weren't you? I thought you'd be delivering for an hour or so, yet."

"Demon attack near Compton," he told her. "We don't deliver to outlying areas when there's a demon attack – it's company policy to keep us safe."

Catriona narrowed her eyes as she thought about the implications of this, and the beginnings of an idea took shape in her mind.

"So, how will Renjaf get his stuff?"

"Well, if they catch the demon tonight, I'll have to go out there tomorrow, instead."

"What if they don't catch the demon that quickly?"

"They usually do," Jacob said, not sure where his friend was going with this.

"Yes, but sometimes it can be days, can't it?"

"Sometimes," Jacob agreed.

"So, what would happen to Renjaf's delivery if you couldn't get through?"

"Then he'd get a magical message telling him his stuff is being held securely in Compton ready for him to collect at his convenience."

"Or, I suppose, *inconvenience,* in his case," Cat mused.

Jacob laughed, "You're not wrong! He gave our reception workers a right earful the last time. He hates leaving his tower."

"Could he authorise someone else to pick up his delivery on his behalf?" she wondered.

"In principle, yes," Jacob agreed, nodding, "but I don't think he has anyone to ask. I mean, who's going to help out that grumpy old miser?"

"I am!" Cat declared. She glanced at her timepiece and did a rough calculation in her head. "His tower isn't all that far as the falcon flies. If I'm quick, I should have time to fly there, get his permission, fly back and deliver his stuff by nightfall!"

"You're not serious!"

"Of course I am! Think about it: you said yourself he hates leaving his tower. If I save him the trouble, get him his delivery on time – within a few hours, anyway – he might just be grateful enough to give me *Shifting Stars*!"

"But how will you carry his stuff from the town centre to his tower?"

"Easy! I'll just shove it all in my pocket dimension. I'm getting better at that."

"Cat," Jacob broached, carefully, "I don't want to dampen your enthusiasm, but the way our clothes keep popping in and out of your pocket dimension, I'm not sure it's as stable as you'd like to think."

Catriona smiled, moved over to Jacob and, to his astonishment, kissed him full on the lips. She broke the kiss, shifted her head slightly and whispered in his ear, "It's so sweet that you still think those were accidents."

Jacob stepped back and gasped, "They were deliberate?"

Cat nodded.

"All of them?"

"Yes!" she assured him. "Well," she amended, "most of them. It'll be fine…probably. As long as I don't try it too close to any major sources of wizard magic."

"Such as Renjaf's tower?"

"Oh, Jacob!" she cried. "Don't worry so much! I'll land a short distance away, take his stuff out of my pocket dimension and carry it up the garden path, so to speak. What could possibly go wrong? Look, I'd better go."

Never one to stand in her way, Jacob simply wished her luck.

*****

In the end, gentle reader, my mother's dimensional magic was never put to the test that day, because unfortunately, she had underestimated how stubborn old Renjaf really was. She had already returned many times to tend his grounds, grow the flowers, clean his pond and even reshape and repair his stone walls, all with her druid magic, but through it all, the stone wall that was Renjaf himself remained unmoved.

She offered to get his delivery for him. He refused. She offered to make sure his next five, ten, twenty demon-affected deliveries got through. He still refused. She said she was prepared to do it even if it was a Greater Demon from the lower planes, and it meant risking her life just to bring him a few groceries. Still, he refused.

"But that means you'll have to get it yourself," she pointed out, "and you hate leaving your tower!"

"Yes," he agreed, "I do! But I'd rather do that than accept help from you or anyone else! But by all means, keep coming back here with more harebrained ideas on how to win me round."

"Why not just tell me what you want and then I can do whatever it is?"

"Because what I want is to keep denying you. I want you to keep coming here, trying your heart out to get that book and I want to be here, standing in your way every time."

"But…but why would you do that?"

"Because I might not be able to see much, these days, but I can see the pain on your face very clearly. Because I enjoy seeing that look. Because knowing I am standing in the way of your dreams and ambitions, the way everyone stood in the way of mine, gives me life! And if the occasional trip into town means I get all that, then it's a price I'm willing to pay, and you will never, ever get what you want!"

With that, he once again slammed the door in her face. Hard.

*****

Well, that was it for my mother. She had tried to be kind; she had tried to help. She had shown, I freely confess, gentle reader, far more patience than I would have in her place. Now she was done. Renjaf was a bitter, twisted, horrible old man, and she was done playing nice. She was angrier than she had ever been in her life, but through that anger came a smile – a dark, dangerous smile – because he had made a mistake.

Logically, if Renjaf wouldn't give her the book, she'd just have to take it. Unfortunately, the wizard's tower had excellent defences against intruders, and it would take her some time to probe for weaknesses and find a way to sneak in. To do that, though, she would

41

need the recluse to leave his home – her druid magic may be growing, but she didn't fancy going up against an enraged wizard. Up until now, Cat had been unable to imagine anything making Renjaf leave his tower, but he had just told her that whenever there was a demon attack, he would definitely do exactly that, just to spite her. So, it was clear that this was precisely what she needed: another demon attack.

*****

"And how exactly do you plan to arrange that?" Jacob demanded, later, when she told him her idea. "Make a pact with a wizard who's an expert in summoning demons? Put innocent people in danger just so you can get your book?"

"No, of course not," Cat replied, "but that demon clause in your contract covers any kind of demon, not just the dangerous ones, right?"

Jacob insisted they were all dangerous, but Cat disputed that.

"What about Tricksters?" she asked. "They're more of a pest and a nuisance than dangerous, wouldn't you say?"

If there was a layer missing in my Great Cosmic Sandwich, gentle reader, it's the Tricksters – the mayonnaise of the cosmic planes. Some people actually liked Tricksters with their pranks and their mischief while others hated them more than hell itself. No-one was sure where they even came from, whether from a higher or lower plane or somewhere else entirely. They didn't appear to have any ill intent beyond causing random acts of chaos that they seemed to find hilarious. They're like that relative or co-worker who adores practical jokes and doesn't seem to understand that not everybody thinks they're funny. And like those practical jokes, they can on rare occasions get out of hand and go dangerously wrong, which is why they are legally classed as demons.

"Tricksters could be enough to stop my deliveries – there have been instances of them stealing parcels before – but it's entirely discretionary on the part of the delivery person."

"I can work with that," said Cat.

"But how do you propose to summon a Trickster?" Jacob asked.

"Tricksters aren't really summoned. They just appear because they feel like it."

42

"So again, how—"

"—Don't you see?" gasped an exasperated Catriona. "I don't need to summon a Trickster..." she shapeshifted in front of her friend.

At about four feet tall with skin the colour and texture of coral, bulbous, squid-like head with tentacles for hair and a mischievous grin, Jacob had to admit she did make a pretty convincing Trickster demon.

"I can become one!" Cat finished, redundantly. "All I have to do is run around Compton like this for a couple of days, and people will think there's a real Trickster."

She changed back to her usual self. She didn't much like being a Trickster demon, but she would do it if it meant she could finally get her hands on *Shifting Stars*.

"I don't even need to do anything much. Maybe knock the odd rubbish bin over, grab people's washing off the line and swap it with next door's. Silly things; nothing dangerous. And if it just so happened to be a day when you're supposed to be delivering to Renjaf..."

"...Then he'll leave his tower and come into town," Jacob concluded. "But you can't be in Compton and at his tower at the same time," he pointed out.

"Don't need to be," she countered. "You know what it's like when a Trickster turns up – people start blaming it for everything!"

She was quite right, gentle reader, and it's still the same a thousand years later. A gust of wind blows some rubbish bins over, it's the Trickster. A freak rain shower ruins a garden party, or someone misplaces their keys, it's the Trickster. That's people for you – all this time, all the progress, and they never really change.

"So, what exactly is your plan?" Jacob wondered, with some trepidation.

"Well, I realise my plans don't always work perfectly..." she began.

"How very self-aware of you!" Jacob returned. That earned him a playful shove.

"...and I'm keen to make you completely blameless in all this," she continued, ignoring his remark.

"That would be appreciated."

"So, I'm thinking, what if you planned to deliver as usual – at your discretion – and the 'Trickster' stole something from

43

you…something that would make it absolutely impossible for you to complete your deliveries?"

When Cat outlined the rest of her idea, Jacob told her, "That has got to be the most ridiculous radical plan I've ever heard in my life." He grinned. "Sounds great, let's do it!"

"Ridiculous radical plan," Cat echoed. "I like that!"

It had a good ring to it, she decided.

Catriona rewarded Jacob's support in the bedroom that night, and a few days later, the day before Renjaf's next delivery was due, Catriona and Jacob set their plan in motion.

A 'Trickster' did indeed appear in Compton and start causing mischief. Jacob delivered as usual, despite having to track down a few items that went 'missing' from his cart. (Actually, hidden by Catriona in pre-arranged places.) Jacob was commended for his efforts and reminded that he need not make his deliveries the next day if the Trickster were still around. Jacob said he was determined to go anyway – after all, it was only a Trickster out there, wasn't it?

That first day, the Trickster was tolerated as people simply hoped it would get bored and go away, but by the second day, they'd decided enough was enough and did what people always did in these situations: call in a demon hunter.

Demon hunters loathe Trickster cases. With all the second-hand rumours and false sightings flying around, getting to the truth is almost more trouble than it's worth. Usually, some novice demon hunter is sent in to sort it out, both because none of the more experienced ones can be bothered and because they had to do it when they were novices. In fact, by Catriona's time, it had become a rite of passage for some young demon hunters. Especially ones who felt they had something to prove.

Chapter 7

The second day of the Trickster attack on Compton was the day the rains came, although Cat and Jacob both knew it was neither a real Trickster nor a real attack. It was, however, real rain, in case you were wondering. Weather notwithstanding, Jacob set out on his deliveries as usual, 'intending' to do his full rounds, including going all the way out to Renjaf's tower. Along the way, however, true to Catriona's 'prediction,' he managed to lose his horse. Naturally, everybody would blame the Trickster demon, as they always did in these cases, and in a way, they were right. Just not in the usual way. The horse was, in fact, not really a horse at all, but Catriona herself.

Where was his real horse, you may ask, gentle reader?

Well, that morning, my mother had got up early, taking her 'sort-of-Jacob' form and 'stealing' Bonnie. If anybody happened to see them that morning, in the dark, from a distance, it would not arouse any suspicion. She had considered stealing the horse as the Trickster, but the last thing she wanted was to attract the attention of the demon hunter she had heard was in town.

The previous evening, when going over the plan, she had asked Jacob to draw up a list of all the locations in and around Compton that he would look for Bonnie if she ever wandered off. Places where a horse could be safely left for a few hours.

Now, having been 'stranded,' he could still make deliveries within the boundaries of the town itself, though it would obviously take longer, while at the same time 'looking' for his horse. But Renjaf's delivery was out of the question, so he simply took his packages back to the depot and ensured that a message was sent. During the day, as he did his rounds, Jacob planned to 'look' for Bonnie in all the places he usually would, making sure that he 'found' the correct one as late as possible.

Meanwhile, Catriona made sure that the Trickster was seen all over Compton that morning, never staying in one place for too long. It wasn't easy, staying two steps ahead of the demon hunter all that time. She had nearly been caught on one occasion, already, but had managed to give her the slip by running around a corner, shapeshifting into her red-banded falcon form and flying away.

Around midday, Cat decided she had pushed her luck enough for one day and, seeing an inn up ahead, she decided to stop for a drink and a bite to eat. Cat rolled her eyes at the tacky name *'FaerWay Tavern'* – obviously making a 'clever pun' out of her Faery heritage. The sign – a nonsensical tiny winged Faery hovering above a road – was even worse, and as a rule, she would refuse to go inside on principle. But going anywhere else would waste time she didn't have, and she really was famished, so she stuck to her plan.

When she stepped outside again, she began walking, searching for a suitably secluded spot to shift to her falcon form once more, so she could quickly fly to Renjaf's tower to watch for him leaving. She had to walk quite a distance away from the town centre, as the early afternoon was a busy time in Compton. It didn't matter that the Trickster wouldn't be around the rest of the afternoon; no doubt the rumour mill would be enough to keep the demon hunter busy.

Unfortunately, Catriona was so busy checking all around to make sure no-one would see her, that she failed to look where she was putting her feet and stepped right into a demon trap. A small bubble of magic surrounded her, keeping her inside.

"No, no, no!" she cursed herself. "I don't have time for this!"

She tried to use her druid magic but cut off from nature as she was, it wouldn't respond. Nothing they had taught her at wizard college would help her in this situation, either. Attempts to retrieve her staff from her pocket dimension also failed to yield results, not that she could have used it, anyway. Even if she could unlock its power, when her Angel spoke of a 'dire emergency of worldwide cataclysmic proportions,' it was unlikely that 'getting out of a demon trap that you blundered into and is only there because you're running around, pretending to be a Trickster,' is quite what they had in mind.

Fortunately, the demon hunter came by before long to check on her trap. She cut quite the imposing figure, dressed all in white from her tight-fitting top and short woollen skirt over white leggings that were just visible before disappearing inside long white boots that finished over the knee. The only splashes of colour were a silver-embroidered, purple leather mask that covered the upper half of her face, just leaving her mouth free, and a matching bandana tied around her neck. By her side was a large, ferocious-looking leopard.

The demon hunter looked Catriona up and down, then finally spoke not to her, but to her leopard.

"Well, Shyleen," she sighed, taking a beer bottle out of a pocket, popping the cap and taking a good, long swig, "looks like we've got ourselves another one."

"Hi, any chance of getting me out of here?" Cat asked with a sheepish grin, feeling incredibly embarrassed at having been so careless.

The demon hunter scowled and took another drink.

"I suppose you're going to blame the Trickster like the last one?"

"The Trickster?" Cat wondered, then quickly seized the excuse she'd been offered. "Oh yes, that's right," she giggled, "the Trickster, erm, pushed me in here."

The demon hunter drank some more. She seemed unconvinced.

"Twice in half a day, that's already wearing thin. Personally, I think you people just need to watch where you're going!"

Cat decided honesty was probably the best policy if she was going to get out of this before it was too late, so she confessed that she had, indeed, just stepped into the trap by mistake.

"I knew it!" cried the demon hunter. "The gods only know how you people manage it! The last one, at least he had an excuse, carrying all that stuff. What were you doing, daydreaming?"

Catriona spread her hands, helplessly. "Pretty much, yeah. Sorry. So, any chance of getting me out of here? I don't mean to be rude, but there's, erm, somewhere I need to be, really quite urgently."

"Oh yeah?" The demon hunter shot back, taking one more swig from her bottle. "Well I have a Trickster to catch really quite urgently, but instead I end up wasting half my time chasing rumours and the other half rescuing townsfolk from my demon traps!"

Cat was getting really desperate and frustrated. Yes, she'd blundered into one of her traps. Yes, it was stupid and careless. Yes, she had definitely wasted this young woman's time, but she needed to get out, and she needed to get out now.

The demon hunter's eyes narrowed, shrewdly. "How do I know you're not really a demon yourself?"

"What?" Cat forced a laugh. "What do you mean?"

"Well, there's a Trickster demon running around here, somewhere," said the demon hunter, intending to take another drink, but discovered her bottle was empty. She held it up to the light and peered inside as if to check if she'd missed any and got a drop in her eye for her trouble. She swore and turned away for a moment, lifted up her mask and used the corner of her bandana to wipe her eye. When she turned back, her mask was back in place.

"I was chasing it, earlier," she continued. "Thought I had it cornered. Next thing I know there's a bird with weird markings on its leg, and the Trickster's vanished somewhere."

Cat tried to suppress a panicked look. "What, erm, what's that got to do with me?"

"Well, I don't know. All I know is there's a girl stuck inside a trap that's supposed to catch a Trickster. So that gets me wondering: Maybe you're not really a girl at all. If a Trickster demon can turn into a bird, what else can he turn into? Things aren't always what they seem, believe me, I know! So, as I say, maybe you really are a girl, or maybe you're really a Trickster demon that's just pretending to be a girl. How am I to know, eh?"

Catriona's pulse was beating rapidly. This demon hunter was so, so close to the truth. Too close. She didn't know what to say, what to do. Fortunately, she was saved from having to think of anything.

With a flourish, the demon hunter pocketed her empty beer bottle, and disarmed the trap, allowing Catriona to step free, although she was so nervous by now, she could barely stand up.

"Nah!" the demon hunter said, dismissively. "Only messing with ya! Of course you're not a demon! I mean, come on: shapeshifting magic? Pfft! As if!"

"Yeah," Catriona laughed, allowing her nervous tension to flow out of her body. "As if!"

"I should know better, really. The rumours in this place are out of hand already, without me giving you lot any more ideas! Honestly, if I were to believe all the stories, the Trickster would have to be in two places at once. Fortunately, thanks to my link with Shyleen here," she indicated her leopard companion, "I can be, too."

"Well, if it helps, I'm not really from Compton," Cat assured her, secretly delighted that her ruse had worked so well and sparked so many false rumours. "Just passing through, so they're not actually 'my lot,' and I definitely won't be spreading any daft rumours about shapeshifting Tricksters."

"Thanks for that, at least," said the demon hunter, "and sorry about the wind-up job. You must have thought I was totally mad and drunk to believe such a thing."

"To be fair," Cat smiled, "you are drunk."

"Well, of course I'm drunk! You'd have to be mad to do this job sober!" the demon hunter quipped. "Anyway, didn't you say you have to be somewhere?"

"Yes, I do," Cat agreed. "Shame. It was actually kind of fun meeting you."

"You have a strange idea of fun."

"Oh, you have no idea how I get my kicks around here…er…I'm sorry, I got your leopard's name, but not yours."

"Mandalee," she replied.

"I'm Catriona. Cat to my friends."

"Ah, now that explains it," Mandalee said.

"Explains what?" asked Cat.

Mandalee stroked Shyleen's head and replied, "I've always got along really well with cats!"

Cat grinned and hurried away, this time making absolutely sure she was out of sight before shapeshifting to her falcon form and taking to the sky. She knew Renjaf would have received his message about his waiting packages by now and if he were true to form, he would want, however grudgingly, to leave his tower and get them as soon as possible. Cat just prayed she wasn't too late. She couldn't pull this stunt a second time, and she had no other ideas of how she was going to get her hands on *Shifting Stars*. Without that, her research into her Angel, her staff and everything related to it were at a dead end. Frankly, this research was such a part of her now that she couldn't imagine what she would do with her life without it.

This was so important to her, it felt as though she was burning inside. She felt like she was on the verge of a new phase in her life, and it was imperative she did not miss her chance. Renjaf's tower had been in her way for too long already. Catriona thought about the things Renjaf had said to her last time. He wasn't merely stubborn, and it wasn't that he didn't understand or care about what this meant to her as he had first suggested. No. He knew, he understood perfectly, and he was actually enjoying her suffering. She had no idea what had happened to make him that way, but she was done feeling sorry for him. Now she felt only the burn.

She let these feelings fuel her, energise her for what she was about to do. This was it: this time she was getting that book, even if she had to destroy Renjaf's tower to get it. Because she'd figured it out, now – that demon hunter had given her the answer. No matter what wizard magic Renjaf had in place, defending against intruders, there was one thing he couldn't possibly have prepared for because nobody believed it existed. Mandalee had practically seen it, and she still didn't believe it: shapeshifting. But not just changing her own shape. Her magic had grown significantly through working on Renjaf's land, and she'd already done what she needed to do. She'd just been doing it backwards.

Chapter 8

The rain that had met the day in Compton was very much present in the outlying areas, too, which helped Cat in her reconnaissance of Renjaf's tower. Muddy footprints leading away from the tower told her that the wizard had already left the building. That was good news in one way because she wanted the tower empty for what she was about to do – she had no wish to harm him. In another way, however, getting there late meant she did not have as much time to do what she was about to do, as she would have liked. Still, it was now or never.

This was a turning point in my mother's history. You see, gentle reader, what Catriona had finally realised, was that when she had been trying to think of a way to affect entry, she had been thinking too much like a wizard. It was how she had been taught to think in college, but she now knew those lessons were valuable in only one respect: they were an excellent example of what not to do. She didn't need to penetrate the shields and wards that were attached to the stonework of the building. That's what a wizard would try to do. For all their fancy tricks, much of wizard magic came down to power and pure mathematics. To penetrate the shield, the power of the attack would have to be greater. Different types of magical attack might work better than others, as shields tended to be unequal in their resistances, but ultimately, it was all about the numbers.

Druid magic was different. It wasn't about power. If Catriona could use her druid magic to reshape and repair his stone walls, then she could use that same magic to tear them down.

Catriona inhaled a few deep breaths and took a firm grip on her staff. She wasn't going to pull power from it, but it did serve as an aid to concentration and focus. She sent forth her magic, not quickly and violently, but slowly and gently. In moments, the stonework began to reshape itself, growing softer and eroding away as if the building had not seen any maintenance for centuries. At last, with an almighty crash, the tower collapsed under its own weight.

'What about the shields?' you may ask, gentle reader.

Well, you see, the shields were attached to the surface of the building, but when the building was reduced to rubble, that surface area grew exponentially. Through it all, the magical shield tried its best, but ultimately, there simply wasn't enough of it to go around, and so there

51

were gaps. Catriona sent her locator spell through the remains of the building until it found *Shifting Stars*. It was buried beneath the rubble, but that was OK, she just asked the debris very nicely if it would mind moving a bit more in one place, allowing her to retrieve it. The rubble didn't much care what shape it took, so it was a simple task to move it aside. When Cat finally got her hands on the book, she found it somewhat worse for wear, but again, that was no problem, she just used her magic again. It was all just shapeshifting when she got right down to it; she just needed the book to return to the shape and condition it was in a moment ago when it was sitting on a bookshelf, and soon enough it was. It was all a question of imagination and explaining to Blessed Alycia what it was she wished to do. The Mother of Nature freed up a tiny portion of the energy she was holding in, which was channelled through Catriona, used to accomplish what she needed and then recycled back into the cosmos.

It felt exhilarating – both the magical achievement itself and the fact that she finally had the book she had been seeking for so long – and her staff itself seemed to reward her with a rather pleasant jolt. It had done something similar when she had unlocked its first layer of security, she remembered. At the time Catriona wasn't sure if she'd imagined it – now she was sure she hadn't. The staff definitely seemed to be 'rewarding' her when she moved a step closer to understanding it.

She carefully slipped the book into her pocket dimension and took a moment to bask in her feelings. That was a mistake because before she knew what was happening, she was being thrown to the ground by wizard magic. Renjaf had returned.

In the split second that she was falling, she was able to persuade the vegetation to move and grow rapidly enough to cushion her fall. She couldn't afford to surrender to unconsciousness. Still, she was held there, hands pinned beneath her, unable to move a muscle.

"What the hell have you done!" Renjaf demanded. "That was my home!"

Only a day ago, she would have talked to him, tried to reason with him, but things were different now – s*he* was different now. She had woken something within herself. Call it stubbornness, call it confidence, call it arrogance, call it madness – she would be accused of all of these in the years that followed. But whatever name one might wish to give it, she was done playing nice with those who refused to co-operate.

Laying there, she focussed her mind and reached out to the grounds that surrounded her, because the tower might have been his home, but the grounds were hers. He had neglected them where Cat had tended them. Through his inaction, they had been choking. Through her actions, they were thriving. Now, when she needed their help, she scarcely needed to ask. Tree branches reached out to restrain him, and vines snaked through the grass to tie his hands, for wizard magic had a weakness: it relied on the user weaving intricate patterns in the air, writing in the language of magic. But what if he couldn't move his hands? What if his hands were tied? Well then, his powers were severely diminished, if not entirely absent.

She felt him try to attack her with powerful mental magic, but her link with Pyrah meant he was wasting his time. Time he didn't have. Plants grew tall around him, pressing, squeezing, choking him even as Catriona was released. She stood and mentally thanked nature for her help, but enough was enough, so they loosened their grip.

Striding purposefully towards Renjaf's feebly struggling, green-covered form, she said, "You brought this on yourself, old man. All I wanted was the book. That's all. Just one book. I have no idea what happened to you that made you the way you are, and frankly, I don't care anymore. You've pushed me too far, and this is the result. Stuck in the undergrowth like an oversized garden gnome and your tower in ruins at your feet. I'm not going to apologise for this, and I'm not going to ask for an apology from you because I know you won't mean it. What I am going to do is what I came here to do in the first place, and as it stands, my work here is only half done."

With that, she spun around, raised her staff, and channelled her magic once more, allowing Renjaf to watch wide-eyed as his tower gradually knitted itself back together, reverting to its former shape and dimensions until it was impossible to tell anything had ever happened to it in the first place. As if to mock the wizard's abilities, even his shields were back in place. When he later probed them with his magic, they would assure him that they were never breached, which was technically accurate. It was hardly their fault that his tower had decided to change its shape.

With a glance from Catriona, the greenery retreated from the wizard, freeing him once more.

"How did you do that?" he breathed in awe.

"You can puzzle over that in your own time," Cat replied. "My time is better spent elsewhere – I've wasted enough of it here already. I suggest you go inside; it's quite safe. Everything should be as you left it…more or less."

"I'll get you for this!" he swore, glowering at her.

Cat snorted a laugh and shook her head in disbelief.

"You really want to threaten me now? I just beat you with both hands literally behind my back! As I say, I've wasted enough of my time here already, and I'll waste no more. I will be leaving now; don't even think about trying anything."

With that, she strode down his path, all greenery parting before her. The gate opened as she approached and shut itself behind her. She wanted to shift into a red-banded falcon and return to Compton as quickly as possible, but she wouldn't do that until she was definitely out of his sight. She had learned that lesson already today. As soon as she was positive that she was well hidden from Renjaf, she paused just for a moment and asked the wind to carry her voice to his ears.

"Almost forgot," she said. "I suggest you get someone to tend your grounds every now and again. I won't be coming back, and they might get a bit cranky if you neglect them again."

She flew back without incident to Compton and the place where she'd left Jacob's horse – literally, the last place her friend would look for her. It was one of several disused barns on the outskirts of Compton, dating back to when the town used to be farmland.

This time, she made absolutely sure there was no demon hunter around when she shapeshifted to her 'delivery boy' form so that she could pass as Jacob while she brought Bonnie outside where her friend could 'find' her.

It was imperative that any passers-by wouldn't recognise Catriona. That could lead to awkward questions about what she was doing with Jacob's horse when it had supposedly been stolen by the Trickster. Catriona tied Bonnie up safely outside, and then, moving away from the immediate area, chose another old barn as the place to discreetly change back. She smiled at the sight of the Trickster tracks she had left, earlier. Mandalee was right – she did have a strange sense of fun, sometimes.

Flushed with a newfound confidence, she visualised what she wanted to do next: Reach into her pocket dimension, throw in her boy clothes, shapeshift and immediately clothe herself in her customary red wizard's robes, all in one fluid movement. As she initiated the process, however, a small spider brushed her left ear, causing her to reflexively jump forward while trying to brush it off. In doing so, she once again failed to watch where she was going and fell into a demon trap, mid-process.

That, gentle reader, left my mother still looking a lot like Jacob, completely naked except for a strategically placed wooden staff with a large blue crystal on top. And just as before, cut off from nature, her magic simply refused to work. She was stuck. Again.

Chapter 9

Isn't it always the way, gentle reader?

There you are, feeling on top of the world, flush with success and the next thing you know, you're stuck in a trap with nothing but a stick to protect your dignity.

Catriona was grateful for the cover of the late evening darkness; it was the only cover she was going to get until the demon hunter, Mandalee, came along to rescue her. That was not a meeting she was looking forward to, but she knew it was the only way she was getting out.

Eventually, the young woman in white strode into view, leopard by her side. Her expression seemed to fluctuate between annoyed and amused.

"Hi," Cat-as-Jacob said sheepishly with a small wave.

"I can't wait to hear your explanation," Mandalee said, hands on hips. "It had better be spectacularly good if you expect me to let you out!"

"It isn't easy to explain."

"I bet it isn't!" Mandalee returned. "Well, while you're trying to work that one out, let me ask you an easier one: Do you have a brother?"

"A brother?" Cat frowned. "No, why?"

"Because you look a lot like some guy I fished out of one of my traps this morning."

Cat thought for a moment, and then realised who she must mean.

"Was he carrying a load of packages by hand because he'd lost his horse, by any chance?"

Mandalee nodded. "So you do know him."

"Yes, that'll be Jacob," Cat replied, "and no, I'm not his brother."

"Then how come you look so much alike?"

"Ah, well, you see, now we're back to the part that isn't easy to explain."

"I can leave you for a while to figure it out," Mandalee offered.

"No!" Cat cried. "Wait! You can't leave me like this, it's a bit cold to be naked."

"Better talk quickly, then."

"Alright, I'll tell you, but you're not going to believe me."

"Try me."

56

"Alright then, well, for a start, I'm not really a boy, I'm a girl."

All trace of humour left Mandalee's face. "What?" she demanded.

"I said you wouldn't believe me, but it's true: I'm really a girl."

For some reason Catriona couldn't fathom, Mandalee looked furious. "Are you trying to be funny? Why the hell would you say something like that? I've got a good mind to leave you in there for the rest of the week!"

"But it's true!" Cat protested. "We met earlier," she pressed on, quickly, seeing the demon hunter turn as if to walk away. "I'm Catriona. Cat. You said you always got on really well with cats, present situation excepted!"

Mandalee turned back around, her anger gradually giving way to puzzlement.

"You're serious?"

Cat nodded.

"Not taking the piss?"

"No, why would I?"

"You honestly don't know?"

"I'm sorry, I really don't know what else I can say," Cat admitted, "but if you let me out, I can show you."

"Alright," Mandalee accepted, "but if I find out you really are taking the piss, well, let's just say Shyleen here's feeling pretty hungry."

With that warning, she deactivated her trap. Cat immediately felt her connection to nature restored and breathed deeply before shifting back to her natural form, ensuring her long hair fell strategically over her breasts.

Mandalee stared, wide-eyed and open-mouthed.

"Sorry," she apologised, turning away, "but if you're really a girl why would you ever want to—" she seemed to catch herself, "—I mean, how did you change like that? Obviously, it's shapeshifting magic, but don't you lose a year of your life whenever you do it or something?"

Cat looked at her, quizzically. "You've been reading too many books! Basically, it's something I've learned to do with my druid magic. Speaking of changing, do you mind if I put some clothes on? People don't usually get to see this much of me unless you buy me a drink first," she quipped, trying to ease the tension.

"Of course!" The demon hunter gasped. "Sorry, it's just a lot to take in, erm…" she started to take off her backpack, "…I think I might have something you could throw on—"

"—No need for that," Cat interrupted. "If you could just hold my staff for a minute…" she held it out with one hand as she started to open her pocket dimension with the other.

When Mandalee, trying not to look at Cat's now fully exposed body, wrapped her hand around the staff, there was a flash of magic as they briefly held it simultaneously, sending them and the staff flying apart. At the same time, Catriona's clothes fell out of her pocket dimension, along with *Shifting Stars*, and Mandalee's clothes fell in – even the mask and bandana were gone. Now the tables were turned, with a naked Mandalee desperately clinging to the staff to try and hide something Catriona had really not expected to see.

All at once, Cat put two and two together. Things Mandalee had said, the mask hiding her face, her reaction to the idea that Cat might be 'trying to be funny' when she said she was really a girl. Mandalee had – biologically speaking – been born male, or at least with a male body. Something the demon hunter was obviously not happy about.

Catriona was abject in her apology. "Mandalee!" she cried. "I am so sorry!"

She immediately grabbed the demon hunter's stuff from her pocket dimension and handed it to her, gently. She turned her back and retrieved her staff as Mandalee dressed. Cat didn't trust herself to throw them straight on with her magic, nor did she believe that would be polite or acceptable to Mandalee.

"That's what you were going to say, before, isn't it? That's why you were furious, because you thought I was…but I wasn't, I swear! I had no idea! Dear gods, I had no right to 'out' you like that. I would never—"

Mandalee placed a hand on Cat's shoulder and turned her around. "It's OK," she assured her. "I believe you. I've mostly learned to pass, and the clothes and mask help with that," she was fully dressed, now, apart from her mask, which she was about to put on, "but without them…" she trailed off.

Cat gently touched her arm to stay her hand. "You don't have to hide your face," she said, "not from me, and you shouldn't for anyone else, either. It's not right."

"It's just easier when I'm interacting with people," Mandalee shrugged. Even so, she didn't put her mask back on. "Which, to be honest, I do as little as possible."

Cat asked if would like to go somewhere and talk, but Mandalee pulled a face at that.

"Well at least let's sit down here," Cat suggested.

"I don't know, the ground's still pretty wet from all the rain," Mandalee pointed out.

"Oh, I can soon sort that out," she replied dismissively and used her magic to encourage the grass, trees and plants to drink a bit quicker, effectively creating a dry patch large enough for two women and one leopard to sit in comfort.

"Shyleen says 'thanks,'" Mandalee said with a smile.

Pulling on her experience of communicating sympathically with Pyrah, Cat tried to project, '*Welcome, respect, friendship.*'

Mandalee's eyes widened in surprise. "What was that? You spoke to her?"

"Well, sort of," Cat allowed. "I call it sympathic communication. It isn't easy to explain."

"Like how you end up naked, cross-gendered and stuck in a demon trap?" Mandalee laughed.

Cat joined in the laughter, "Yes, like that," she agreed.

"Shyleen said it's not like when I do it – I'm a Cleric of Nature, I speak just about every major animal language telepathically. She says she didn't hear her language but still understood what you were trying to convey."

"Well, that's a better explanation than I could have given you," Cat admitted.

"Don't worry, her explanations are a lot better than mine, too. She's a very philosophical cat, our Shyleen. She's taken a definite liking to you and approves of our friendship."

"Oh, so we're definitely friends now, then?" Cat smiled.

"Shyleen says we are, so we must be," Mandalee insisted with a grin. "She's never wrong."

"Well then, far be it from me to argue." She held out a hand, which Mandalee shook, warmly. "Glad to meet you, Friend," she said.

"Likewise, Friend," the demon hunter affirmed. "Dear gods, I can't remember the last time I felt so free talking to someone, without worrying about," she gestured vaguely to indicate herself, "you know."

Cat waved that aside and with a wink, she quipped, "Hey, I showed you mine, you showed me yours!"

Mandalee snorted. "We've certainly left ourselves with very little to hide from each other. How did that actually happen, anyway? Any ideas?"

"Ah, you gave me the final piece of the puzzle I needed to put it together."

"I'm all ears," said Mandalee.

"Not from what I saw!" Cat remarked.

Mandalee gave her a shove for her trouble and tried to look intimidating while stifling her laughter.

Cat then explained about her pocket dimension magic and how, although it was mostly under control, now, she'd had problems with instability in the presence of wizard magic.

"It seems your cleric magic was enough to confuse it, too. Just like your cleric-powered demon trap kept me stuck in a male body."

With a grimace, Mandalee replied, "I know that nightmare all too well. Honestly, if I could shapeshift like you, I'd never go back to this body."

Cat fixed her new friend with a serious look. "Do you really mean that?"

"I've meant it all my life," she replied ruefully. "Unfortunately, miracles don't happen."

"Miracles can happen if people make them happen," Cat countered.

"Nobody has that kind of power," Mandalee insisted with a shake of her head.

"Power isn't everything," Cat returned. "With the right application of knowledge, skill, technique and imagination, people can achieve all kinds of things."

"What are you saying?" Mandalee demanded, her heart rate accelerating. "That you could…" she wiggled her fingers, vaguely.

"Well it'll take a bit more than that," Cat told her with a smile, "and I certainly can't do it right here this minute, but with time and study, I really don't see why it shouldn't be possible."

"Don't do this to me, Cat!" Mandalee pleaded. "Not unless you're sure."

"I'm not sure," Cat admitted, "and I won't attempt anything until I am, but I am confident. Give me time and I honestly, truly believe I'll be able to do it."

Mandalee wrapped her new friend in a huge embrace. "That would be amazing." She broke the hug, held Cat by the shoulders at arm's length, staring into her eyes. "But whether you can do it or not, the fact that you'll try makes us friends for life. That's it, now. You're stuck with me."

"I'll drink to that with pleasure!" Cat declared, then she realised something. "Hey, you don't have a drink with you!"

"I only drink when I'm on duty. I'm done for the night. Let the Trickster do what it will!" she declared.

"Ah," Cat remarked.

"What?" Mandalee asked.

"In the interests of having nothing to hide, there's one thing I haven't told you."

"About the Trickster?"

Cat nodded.

"You know something about it?"

Again, Cat nodded.

"Go on, then. What is it?"

"There isn't one," Cat admitted. "It was just me. All part of my ridiculous radical plan to get this." She held up *Shifting Stars*.

Mandalee screamed with laughter. "You spent two days running around as a Trickster just to get your hands on a book?" She was incredulous.

"Oh, you have no idea what I've been through to get this," Cat replied, ruefully.

Wiping tears from her eyes, the demon hunter stood up and held out a hand to her friend, "I think this story is going to need a drink."

Cat took the hand and pulled herself up. "I thought you said you only drink when you're on duty?"

"I am on duty," she replied, linking arms with Cat and sending a telepathic invitation for Shyleen to join them. "I just caught the Trickster!"

The two friends laughed as they walked together, heading for the *FaerWay Tavern*.

Chapter 10

Serendipity. A beautiful word for a beautiful concept. Through this happy accident, gentle reader, a friendship was born: a friendship for the ages. From this moment, though the paths of their lives might send them apart, they would always find their way back to each other. Only one thing could part them forever, and I know Aunt Mandalee still misses my mother terribly. Having said that, my mother wasn't entirely convinced their meeting was just an accident. She had the strangest feeling it was more than that.

"There is still one mystery," Cat told her friend after she shared her story. They were enjoying a drink outside the *FaerWay Tavern* – for some reason, they didn't allow leopards inside. At least, she hoped it was Shyleen they were objecting to and no-one else.

"What's that?" Mandalee wondered.

"My staff."

"Your staff?"

"Yes, I have no idea why it reacted the way it did when we touched it together before."

"Has another cleric ever held it before?" Mandalee asked.

"Not while I've owned it, no, but it's deeper than that. Mandalee, I don't normally let anyone else touch it!" She trusted Jacob, but she'd never let him get his hands on it. "In fact, come to think of it," she mused, "I'm not even sure why I let you. It just felt…right, somehow."

"Are you saying we were destined to meet, or something?"

Cat shook her head, emphatically. "Not exactly. I'm not really one for destiny as such, but I do have the strangest feeling…"

"What kind of feeling?" Mandalee prompted.

Catriona took a few breaths to consider before responding, "Like somebody wanted us to meet. They didn't make it happen – more like they encouraged it to happen. Like when you introduce two friends to each other, and you hope they'll get along and you're pleased when they do."

"Well, you're a druid, and I'm a Cleric of Nature, so maybe it was Blessed Alycia herself who encouraged it," Mandalee suggested.

"Maybe," Cat allowed. "Anyway," she continued, dismissing it for the moment, "what would life be without a few mysteries?"

"Quiet?"

"You say 'quiet,' but all I hear is 'dull,'" Cat replied, finishing her drink.

Mandalee smiled and downed the remains of hers.

"Why do I get the feeling my life is going to be neither of those things ever again now I've met you?"

Cat spread her hands. "I really can't imagine!"

By this time, Catriona was getting slightly worried about Jacob. She would have expected him to have turned up by now. She sent out a sympathic message to him, conveying a sense of *'searching'* and *'concern.'*

While she waited for a response, she explained to Mandalee that since Jacob had no magic, she had to initiate contact and it took mental effort to sustain it even for a short period. In theory, with another magic user, she believed she could set up a permanent, effortless, two-way sympathic link.

Jacob responded with the concept of *'getting closer'* and *'location query.'*

"He's on his way and wants to know exactly where I am," she translated for Mandalee, then she sent a sympathic message, telling Jacob she was drinking at the rear of the tavern, rather than simply meeting outside as they had planned.

Jacob returned an image that conveyed suitable disgust at her projected image of the culturally offensive sign in front of her: a road or path over which hovered a nonsensical tiny 'Faery,' complete with wings.

Why was it so difficult for some humans to realise that Faery did not have wings; that was Piskeys, their smaller cousins. Except there weren't any anymore.

*****

Long ago, gentle reader, Faery shared their forest homes with Piskeys. Then, gradually, infertility increased, and their numbers began to decline. Nobody knows why. By my mother's time, the last of the winged Piskeys had died around eight hundred years ago, and the species became extinct.

But their legacy did not entirely disappear from Tempestria, because before their fertility problems began, interbreeding with Faery

63

was common, and so modern Faery retained within their bodies, a small sliver of what the Piskeys once were. Their smaller, lighter builds were the primary example, but every now and then, a baby was born with tiny, vestigial wings on their back. The Piskey legacy was stronger in them, which also meant they could not have children.

Sadly, some humans were wilfully ignorant about other cultures, and depicting Faery like Piskeys with wings was an example of this. The way my mother saw it, it was not only insulting to the Faery, but also to the memory of the Piskeys who were no longer around to protest.

*****

Jacob's response told Cat he had correctly deduced that, against her better judgement, she was an actual customer at the appallingly named *FaerWay Tavern* and told her he'd be there in five minutes.

After relaying that to Mandalee, she said, "I don't want to be rude, but do you mind if we drop the conversation for a bit so I can read some of *Shifting Stars*? Having gone to so much trouble to get hold of this book, I'm itching to see if it was worth it."

Mandalee said she didn't mind at all and was curious herself. So, Cat opened the book that was apparently so ridiculed.

*****

The world is wrong, and the stars make no sense.

Catriona and Mandalee shared a look – not the most promising start.

Clerics would have us believe that the cosmos is a plaything of the gods, and not to be understood by mortals. But that is what they said about magic, and yet through study, wizards can now do what clerics said was impossible without recourse to any gods. I put it to you that the world is inherently understandable, conforming to laws that we can begin to formulate. At least it should be.

Yet the stars will not behave.

For a while, they do. Sometimes for long periods, their positions in the heavens are entirely rational, sensible, predictable. Then, every now and again, at seemingly random intervals, there is a Star Shift, and some of them stray off course. The question is: Is something moving the stars, or is something moving our world relative to them? What effect might that have on Tempestria? This is to say nothing of the void storms – the vortex that swirls all around us. That seems to change its pattern at the same time as the Star Shift. Why? What are the void storms? Is there some link between them and the stars? Is the movement of one the cause of the other, or are both symptoms of the same problem?

In this book, I intend to present my evidence and hope to at least begin to answer some of these questions.

*****

I am not going to reproduce the entire book here, gentle reader, for reasons of copyright violation if nothing else. Suffice to say, what followed was mainly annotated diagrams and star charts along with wild, speculative theories about the forces that might be involved. It appeared to be superficially scientific in its approach, but as Mandalee said, "You could probably write a book all about the science of the flight of pink elephants, but that doesn't make them real."

Even Catriona might have been sceptical except for one thing. It was the thing that made her seek out this book in the first place. The other books she had read that referenced *Shifting Stars* if only to point and laugh. References that suggested this book contained a supposedly first-hand account of an event that connected to something very precious to Catriona. After flicking through the book, she found it, right at the end, just as Jacob showed up and joined them.

*****

A figure appeared, glowing with a light that made it hard to see them directly. I could determine neither race nor gender. I thought I could detect a strange aura and a kind of magic that defied identification. The mage produced a small wooden staff, approximately three feet in height, topped with a large blue crystal. I know not from where they got it, save that they seemed to open some kind of rift or perhaps a door to some other reality and simply pulled the staff into our world. This figure invoked some sort of magic on the staff, or possibly through it, and the crystal atop the staff sent a coloured lightshow high into the sky. The void storms twisted and danced in response, and that is when one section of stars changed their position in the heavens.

Who was this figure, and what were they doing? My investigations lead me to believe this has happened many times before. Every time it does, this glowing figure seems to be able to hide from the gaze of almost everyone there present. But among the masses, there is always a Chosen One who can see through their magic. Unfortunately, since they are the sole witness, they are disbelieved and even ridiculed. That is why I have written this book, in hopes that it will touch the minds of those who can see this threat for what it is.

Shifting Stars is not just an academic curiosity, but a warning to all. It is my opinion that whatever this strange magic is, we must find a way to stop it before there are any further such occurrences. For if they continue unchecked, I fear they are going to destroy the world!

*****

Literally bookending one's academic work with 'The world is wrong' and 'They are going to destroy the world' is unlikely to give it much credence, but I'm sure, gentle reader, you will recognise much of this. Catriona and her two friends certainly did.

"That sounds like your Angel with your Crystal Mage Staff," Jacob remarked.

"Yes, it does," she agreed, "and if he's right about that, then I'm not going to be so quick to dismiss the rest of it. I think the conclusion is all wrong, though: I don't believe my Angel is a threat. Not after all they did to mend Quarthonia."

Mandalee concurred, "Why fix a village if you're going to destroy the world?"

"Seems a bit counter-productive," Jacob agreed.

"Question is," Mandalee put in, "was there a star shift on the day you met your Angel?"

"No idea," Cat said. "I wasn't paying attention to that. I was looking at the land. But I certainly intend to find out and also to verify the 'evidence' of star shifts in this book. I'm not going to dismiss it out of hand like most people, but I'm not going to accept it on faith, either. Looks like I have plenty more studying to do."

"Somehow I think you'll cope," Jacob said with a wry smile.

"I think you're right," Mandalee agreed.

Cat gasped, and apologised, "I'm so sorry, you two!" She closed her book and tucked it safely away. "I haven't even introduced you. That's so rude!"

"That's OK," Mandalee assured her. "We met this morning when I fished him out of one of my demon traps, which I'm going to have to start calling 'people traps,'" she added with an annoyed frown, "since so far that's all they've caught."

"I have some ideas about that," Cat told her. Turning to Jacob, she teased, "How could you be so careless? Just watch where you're going!"

"Hey, it's not my fault! The Trickster pushed me in!"

"Oh, that old chestnut!" Mandalee groaned, rolling her eyes.

"Yeah," Cat agreed. "I tried that one the first time."

"I wasn't buying it," Mandalee said, "and it's OK, I know Cat was the Trickster. You don't need to pretend."

"Good to know. Wait – the first time?" Jacob wondered.

With a blush, Cat admitted, "Oh, yeah, I'm actually in no position to wind you up about walking into one of Mandalee's traps – I managed it twice!"

"Twice?" Jacob repeated, suppressing a smile.

"Yep," Mandalee confirmed, "and the second time she did it naked!"

"No!"

"Looking quite a lot like you."

"Oh, this gets better!" Jacob grinned. "Really?"

Cat nodded. "Sat there in my – well, *your* birthday suit."

"With nothing but her staff in her hand," Mandalee added.

"I hope that's not a euphemism!" Jacob quipped.

All three cracked up at that.

When they'd sufficiently calmed down, Jacob asked, "So why'd you do it, Cat?"

"I was distracted by a spider, and my magic got a bit confused by Mandalee's," she explained. "Then, once inside her trap, I was cut off from nature and couldn't do anything."

Jacob shook his head. "No, I mean, why did you push me in Mandalee's trap? That wasn't in the plan!"

"What are you talking about?" Cat frowned. "I didn't push you in that trap, you just blundered in by mistake like I did."

"No," he disputed, "you were running around as the Trickster, and you pushed me in the trap!"

"Wait, are you serious?" Cat asked.

"Yes, of course!"

"No kidding? You're honestly saying the Trickster pushed you in that trap?"

"Yes, really, no kidding! Why are you asking this, Cat? You were there!"

"No, Jacob, I promise you I wasn't."

Mandalee leaned forward, a serious look on her face. "So, Jacob, if the Trickster really did push you in my trap…"

Jacob nodded.

"…and Cat, it definitely wasn't you…"

Cat shook her head.

"…that means, there really is a Trickster loose in Compton!"

Eyes wide, Catriona gasped, "Mandalee, didn't you say something about if you were to believe all the reports of sightings, the Trickster would have to be in two places at once?"

"You're right, I did," the demon hunter confirmed. "Seems I dismissed the reports too easily."

"We have to track it down!" Cat said, resolutely.

"We?" Mandalee wondered. "It's my job, there's no need for you to get involved."

"But it's my fault!"

"How is it your fault?" Jacob asked. "You didn't bring it here."

"Actually, she might have," Mandalee countered. "Tricksters are drawn to pranks and mischief, and with everything Cat's been up to, I'm afraid a real Trickster may have taken it as an invitation to come out and play!"

"That's why I have to help," Cat insisted.

She stood up, ready to spring into action, but she swayed on her feet and had to use her staff to hold herself up. She hadn't realised how tired she was.

"It's getting late, and you're exhausted," Jacob observed.

Catriona smiled weakly.

"I am feeling a bit drained, now you mention it," she conceded. "Big day."

"Go home and rest up," Mandalee advised, reaching out a steadying hand. "You can help me tomorrow if you like. It's not like

68

it's a Greater Demon that's going to drag people down to hell. It's only a Trickster."

Cat agreed and asked where Mandalee was staying.

"Out here," said the demon hunter. "Bit difficult to find a room that allows leopards," she said, stroking Shyleen.

Once again, Cat fervently hoped it was the leopard people objected to.

"Besides, I prefer to be out underneath the stars…even if they are all wrong!"

"I remember what that was like," Cat replied, with a distant, slightly haunted look. "I haven't really done it since the night I met my Angel…since my Mum and Dad…since they were…well…"

Jacob put his arm around her and Mandalee quickly moved the conversation along so her friend wouldn't have to finish that sentence.

"What about your sympathic thing?" she suggested. "You could contact me like that when you're ready to get going."

As an experiment, Catriona projected, '*tired, sleep.*'

"Curious sensation," Mandalee remarked and tried to project back. It took her a few goes, but soon she managed to send, '*night, dreaming*' which Cat took to mean, "Goodnight, sweet dreams."

Cat thought the latter was unlikely since she had never experienced a dream in her life, but she took the sentiment in the spirit in which it was intended.

With that, they exchanged hugs and went their separate ways.

Chapter 11

The next morning, Catriona met up with Mandalee and Shyleen. Shapeshifting into her falcon form, she was able to scout around the town while Shyleen tracked down the Trickster's scent. Now that there wasn't a second Trickster confusing the trail, it made things easier by far. Once they found it, Cat was able to work her magic on the plants to cut off escape routes. Shyleen herded it into one of Mandalee's traps, which, with Catriona's help, she had adjusted to give off an inaudible vibration that would naturally repel distracted mortals, while still attracting lower planar demons. Once captured, the demon hunter used her clerical magic to Banish the Trickster, robbing it of the energy it would need to return to the mortal realm anytime soon.

Mandalee and Cat made a good team. Their skills complemented each other and their sympathic communication, plus the telepathy between Mandalee and Shyleen, helped them work together as one. They didn't know it at the time, but this was only the beginning for them. Soon, they would be working together regularly as the consequences of Catriona's actions caught up with her and changed the course of her life.

*****

Cat, Mandalee and Jacob were all together when the message arrived. It was a magical message from the Council of Wizards. Catriona was summoned to stand before them in Conclave.

Renjaf had filed a formal grievance against her, and this was a hearing to determine the degree of culpability and decide on what, if any, punitive action was warranted.

The Council of Wizards recognised no single leader. Instead, it was governed by a Triumvirate composed of the highest-ranking wizard from each of the three orders of magic: White, Black and Red. The White were primarily concerned with the defence and protection of the people of Tempestria, especially from the harmful effects of magic. The Black were mostly interested in the security and protection of magic, arguably from the harmful effects of people, which often manifested in the form of a lust for power. The Red were focussed on promoting the advancement of magical knowledge and encouraging diversity in magic.

Choosing one of the three magical colours was not compulsory, but it was highly recommended as it gave one a voice on the Council and support in cases like the one Cat was now facing.

*****

Renjaf, not being one to leave his tower unnecessarily, had already given the Council his full testimony that backed up his claim that Catriona Redfletching had attacked him, destroyed his home and stolen his property in the form of one book, namely *Shifting Stars.*

Cat now had the opportunity to give her side of the story. She told the truth, although she did omit anything to do with pretending to be a Trickster, because it wasn't directly relevant, and Jacob's help, to protect him from the consequences of her choices.

Throughout the proceedings, the Red robe leader used her magic to cause a pen to write out a complete record without her having to hold it. Every now and again she spared it a glance as if to check it was working correctly, but generally, she was able to leave it to its own devices. Cat hadn't seen that kind of magic before and tried to distract herself from her own nerves by considering how it might work.

The reactions of the three leaders were in deep contrast to one another. Maia of the White was keen to focus on the 'unprovoked attack' on one of her order. Justaria of the Red argued that it was far from 'unprovoked.' As for Laethyn of the Black, he wasn't remotely interested, saying, "If this young druid were a Black robe, we would have dismissed this Conclave and be calling for a counter-claim."

"Counter-claim? On what grounds?" Maia demanded to know.

"For the obstruction of her growing magical power. As it is, I say we should throw the whole thing out. If we vote, I'm going to rule in her favour, and so are you, Justaria, we both know it, and your vote counts twice, so that's three. It doesn't matter how Maia votes, so let's not waste any more time."

"I appreciate your position," Justaria said, smoothly, "but due process must be observed. You cannot presume to know how Maia or I will vote before we have considered all the facts."

"Thank you, Justaria," Maia said. "I am pleased to know you are taking this matter seriously."

"I strive for balance in all things," Justaria told her colleague. "Especially justice."

Laethyn was incredulous. "You can't be serious, Justaria! You won't guarantee to support one of your own order?" He shook his head in disbelief. "There's loyalty for you."

"That's rich, considering all the in-fighting among those of the Black order!" Maia remarked.

Laethyn ignored her. Instead, to Catriona, he offered, "Don't forget, you have the right of Realignment."

This referred to a mage changing their allegiance from one colour to another. It would not be allowed if this were a trial, but during a hearing like this, she did have that right. "I've already guaranteed my vote either way because I think this whole thing's a farce, but if you switch to the Black, my vote will count double, making your worst possible outcome two for and two against."

In that event, the case would become a trial, leading to a full Council debate. The majority of Black robes would share their leader's view, so all Cat would need was a majority of Red robes on her side, and it wouldn't matter what the White robes thought about it. Any punishment would be likely to be no more than a slap on the wrist.

"Thank you for your support, Master Laethyn," Catriona replied respectfully, "but I'm afraid I am compelled to decline your offer of Realignment."

"You would gain more power our way," Laethyn pointed out.

"Power isn't everything," Catriona shrugged. "I am perfectly willing to place my confidence in the justice of this Conclave as a member of the Red robes of Balance."

"Well said," Justaria approved. "On the other hand, Maia," she continued, addressing her White robe counterpart, "I think our Black robe colleague raises a valid point. I appreciate that you are seeking compensation for the physical damage done to Renjaf and his property. However, consider for a moment the emotional and spiritual damage done in reverse, and in fact, inflicted first, when all Catriona wanted was to borrow a single book. On that basis, I raise the counter-claim that Laethyn proposes."

"What!" Maia exclaimed. "I thought you were on my side a moment ago!"

Justaria spread her hands. "Apologies if I gave you that impression; I am simply trying to achieve a balance. Laethyn," she said to her Black robe colleague, "might I suggest you raise that counter-claim in pursuit of damages against Renjaf on behalf of Catriona?"

With a smile, Laethyn readily agreed, "Anything to poke holes in the White robes' holier-than-thou attitude. Yes, I hereby officially raise that claim."

"Noted for the record," Justaria accepted, her pen scribbling the entry onto the page all by itself.

Turning back to Maia, Justaria said, "Do you want me to support your pursuit of damages against Catriona on behalf of Renjaf?"

"Yes, I do," she affirmed.

"Very well. Now, as Laethyn says, I believe we all know which way both of you will vote in these claims, so that leaves my vote, and of course, in the case against Catriona I get two."

That was one of the benefits of Council membership. In the case against Renjaf, Maia would be the one with two votes. It was a system intended to prevent collusion between any two leaders.

"Now, it is assumed in these cases that the member with two votes will vote the same way twice, but there is nothing in the rules of the Council that says that must be so. Therefore, I propose to split my vote in the grievance against Catriona, while voting in her favour in the counter-claim."

That meant there would be two votes 'for' and two 'against' both claims.

"But that will send both claims out to full Council!" Maia objected.

Justaria nodded her agreement. "Which would be a sad indictment on the three of us if we can't resolve this simple dispute which has, to my mind, already resolved itself."

"Agreed," Laethyn said.

"I don't believe it's right to throw out either claim, because I firmly believe there was indeed damage on both sides, but there is a way we could avoid this deadlock."

"I'm listening," said Maia.

Justaria explained that she was willing to vote twice to support Renjaf's claim against Catriona, if Maia would split her vote, instead. Thereby supporting the counterclaim as well.

"As for sentencing," Justaria continued, "I suggest the following: For destroying Renjaf's tower, Catriona Redfletching will pay damages by rebuilding it. Which she's already done."

The other two nodded their agreement.

"Now, I believe her magical attack on Renjaf was largely in self-defence since he struck first, but his reaction was understandable since she'd just demolished his home. Therefore, she will pay damages in the form of no less than ten days of community service tending his grounds."

"Which she's already done," Maia said, seeing her colleague's line of thought.

"Finally, in the case of the counter-claim, for extreme emotional distress and failing to provide all reasonable assistance to someone in need, as per White robe policy, I suggest Renjaf pay compensation in the form of precisely one book: the aforementioned *Shifting Stars*."

"Which she's already got," Laethyn said.

Justaria nodded. "This way, we acknowledge the culpability of both sides, we avoid needlessly wasting the Council's time and quite frankly," she added, shooting the others a conspiratorial glance, "we look like we know what we're doing!"

The other two agreed to her terms, the Triumvirate formally cast their votes, and the sentences were passed. Catriona stood and bowed, respectfully as Maia and Laethyn left the Council chamber, but Justaria remained behind.

"Catriona, please sit," she said and sat down beside her. "There is one other matter I need to discuss with you, but it needn't involve the others because it's a matter of internal Red order discipline. Your druid magic is interesting to me, and I am happy to see you exploring the potential of your abilities, as it is perfectly in line with our desire for diversity in magic. As you so succinctly put it, 'Power isn't everything.' However, with any new magic, there must be rules, and while you haven't broken the letter of any of them, because they haven't been written yet, I think you know you broke the spirit of their intent."

Catriona nodded. She'd been thinking about this, herself, in the cold light of day and reached the same conclusion. "Shapeshifting into the form of another person: Jacob. Essentially impersonating him. It's identity theft."

"Yes, it is," Justaria agreed. "and I'm glad you see that. Now, I'm not going to be too harsh on this occasion, because I suspect you did it with his consent…"

Cat opened her mouth to object – she didn't want any of this falling on Jacob, it wasn't fair – but Justaria cut her off.

"Don't worry about confirming or denying that. This isn't a hearing; we're just having a chat, and that was pure speculation on my part. The point is, what you did was a misuse of new magical knowledge and could be seen as a violation of the terms of your membership of our order."

A tearful Catriona offered no excuse or defence. She didn't want to lose her membership, nor her voice on the Council. She believed in what the institution stood for and wanted to be a part of that, but Mistress Justaria was right.

"Knowledge is neutral; its application is not," Cat quoted from the Code of Balance.

"I'm pleased to see you take that lesson to heart," Justaria said, kindly reaching out and resting a gentle, reassuring hand on Cat's arm. "As I said, I'm not going to be too harsh with you. You made a mistake, and I can see that you know it. I'm not going to warn you to never do it again, because I'm quite sure you won't. Therefore, I will not revoke your membership of the Red Robes of Balance..." Catriona's relief was palpable, but Justaria wasn't finished. "...but I will be recommending you be expelled from the College of Magic and banned from using its resources in any way. Do you understand?"

Catriona assured her that she did, so Justaria allowed her to leave. Before she reached the exit door, however, Justaria called out her name.

"Officially, this is a punishment," she said. "Unofficially I believe I'm doing you a favour. I don't think the College has a clue how to teach you – there's never been a mage like you before – and I also believe you will never find the knowledge you seek without severing your ties to that institution. Their ways are not your ways. Let your instincts and your research guide you, free yourself to follow where they lead, and I predict an exciting future for you, Catriona Redfletching."

Stunned by this, the only words Cat could find to express herself were, "Thank you!"

They seemed inadequate, but they would have to do.

One day, gentle reader, both would realise just how prophetic Justaria's words had been.

*****

As you may have gathered, I can use Temporal projection magic to see possible future paths, but I have no need of that to foresee my own Conclave. If that surprises you, it shouldn't. The Guardians and I may operate outside Time, but that does not mean we can operate outside the law without the modern-day Council having something to say about it. When that moment comes, I pray I will be as strong as my mother, prepared to accept whatever their decision might be.

And I can only hope for an equally favourable result.

Chapter 12

Having spent so much time on Catriona and introduced Aunt Mandalee, gentle reader, I think it's high time you met my other Aunt, Dreya the Dark.

Dreya's story is well known, as she herself is famous, or infamous, depending on one's point of view. There are many versions of this story, but I promised you that every word I write would be true, and so as I peel back the layers of Time, I can relay the events, effectively, as they happen.

*****

The first significant, documented account of Dreya's life was when one day, not long after the devastating attack on Catriona's Quarthonian home, she casually knocked on the door of the Red wizard, Xarnas. He had recently retired from the Council where he had served for the last five years as Triumvirate representative, succeeded by Justaria. When he answered the door and looked down at the girl on his doorstep, barely a teenager, lost in too-large robes of a Red wizard, she declared, without preamble, that she wished him to train her in magic. Xarnas kindly explained that he had retired.

Dreya replied that she knew that, which meant he now had sufficient time to devote to her training.

Her presumptuous tone caused raised eyebrows. Few adults would speak to him like that, let alone a child. Yet her voice, when she spoke, was calm and quiet. As if she were merely stating a fact that he had simply overlooked.

When he asked, "Why me?"

Her answer was simply, "Because you are the best."

Again, there was no flattery in that statement, no attempt to curry favour. Dreya was just stating a fact. Still, Xarnas wasn't taking on any more students at this time and told her so.

Dreya, in that exact same tone, replied that *of course,* he wouldn't be taking on any *more* students, as training *her* would require all of his focus and attention. That's why she had waited until now when he was done with the distractions of Council business.

Xarnas would later admit that he was curious about this girl from the start. Her calm, controlled manner and absolute confidence that somehow came over as self-assured, not arrogant, were fascinating to him. Still, he was looking forward to his retirement and did not want an apprentice disturbing his peace.

Dreya told him in her matter-of-fact way that he would be taking her as his apprentice, "before this day is done, so you are really just wasting time. But I am patient and will wait until you are ready to make the right choice."

"In that case," he said, "I suggest you make yourself comfortable on my doorstep because you're going to have a very long wait."

To his amazement, Dreya thanked him, politely and promptly sat down.

Xarnas shrugged. He could see no harm in letting her sit there if that was what she wanted. Soon enough, she would get bored and go.

Except she didn't.

Late that evening, he settled down to read a letter he had received from his youngest daughter, Bronwen, away at magic college. From time to time, he would look out of his window and see Dreya sitting there, either reading a book that she had been carrying in her voluminous robes or practising magic. It was distracting enough for Xarnas to learn about his eighteen-year-old daughter's first serious boyfriend – a Faery, no less – when he was sure Bronwen had been a little girl only five minutes ago, without having an impertinent young Faery girl on his doorstep. Yes, he was missing having his daughter around, but that didn't mean he was looking to adopt a new one!

The evening gave way to night, and still, young Dreya sat there. As midnight approached, Xarnas was preparing to retire. He opened his door, and Dreya immediately stood, respectfully.

"Don't you have a home to go to?" he asked.

"Until now, my home has been in the woodlands with my Faery people, but before this day is done, I shall be living here with you. That will maximise the time you have to train me. Travelling from anywhere else would waste time. Obviously, I could teleport here every day, but that would be a waste of power."

This was the first time she had said something that was clearly arrogant nonsense. Teleportation was a highly advanced wizard spell, which was learned only after years of study and practice.

"You don't seriously expect me to believe you can teleport!" he scoffed.

"No," said Dreya, her tone unwavering. "I do not know how to teleport."

"So why would you imply that you did?"

"I did not mean to imply any such thing," she assured him. "My apologies for the misunderstanding. What I meant was, while I do not know how to teleport *yet*, before this day is done, I will."

"The day is almost done, already," Xarnas pointed out. "I highly doubt you can learn teleportation or much of anything else in these last few minutes."

"I know you have doubts," Dreya replied, "but before this day is done, they will trouble you no longer, and your training will begin."

By now, Xarnas was tired and had simply run out of patience. "Very well," he said, "if you're so interested in teleportation, let me show you how it's done."

With that, he wrote the highly complex spell in the air and sent young Dreya more than a hundred miles away to the heart of the nearest Faery woodland community. She would be safe enough there. The Faery would never hesitate to take care of a lost child, no matter how superior and irritating her attitude. Before he could close his door, however, the young girl reappeared in front of him.

"Thank you for the lesson," said Dreya.

Xarnas was stunned. "How did you do that?"

"I spent the day on your doorstep, reading all I could about the magical theory behind teleportation, how it connects with other powers and the spell form required to activate it. Experiencing it from the inside was just the last piece I needed to do it myself."

"Show me," he demanded. "Prove to me you didn't get someone else to teleport you back here. Prove you can truly do it yourself."

And so, she did.

Dreya teleported herself all over the place in front of his eyes and Xarnas' astonishment grew. To learn teleportation like that was incredible. At that moment, he knew his retirement was postponed. He had always enjoyed teaching even the most challenging of students, but this one would be a challenge of an entirely different order. One could search for ten human lifetimes and still never find a student as intelligent, gifted and talented as this one, and she had just turned up on his doorstep. This was an opportunity he could not refuse.

Moving aside, he said, "Please come in, Apprentice Dreya."

Stepping inside, she bowed and replied, "Thank you, Master Xarnas."

No sooner had the Red wizard closed his door than a sound drifted on the air: the sound of the town hall clock striking midnight. Listening to the chimes, he remembered Dreya's prediction that he would accept her as his apprentice 'before this day is done' and he had – just before the stroke of midnight. He stared open-mouthed at the teen who now stood inside his home.

"Speaking of lessons," said Dreya, "I trust you have also learned yours?"

"And that lesson would be…?"

"Never to underestimate me again."

The Red wizard would indeed never again underestimate her, and he firmly believed that anyone who did so in the future would be lucky if they lived to regret it.

*****

It was about three years into Dreya's training, and she continued to surpass Xarnas' wildest expectations. From the very first day, he had made it widely known that Dreya was with him, thinking that her parents or guardians would claim her. No-one ever did, and Dreya herself flatly refused to talk about her past. Her claim that she was from one of the Faery woodland communities didn't exactly narrow it down – there were a dozen such places on the continent of Elvaria alone. So, for those three years, he unofficially adopted her.

She never shied away from hard work, and she never complained when he assigned her tasks and puzzles that were apparently unrelated to magic, seeming to instantly grasp the lesson he was trying to teach her and how that would later apply to her magic. Her questions were astute and challenging, her aptitude unparalleled. She wanted to know everything about how magic worked, down to the smallest detail and she grasped it all, although she wasn't afraid to question assumptions and challenge beliefs.

Through it all, however, there was a puzzle about Dreya that Xarnas simply could not work out. He could sense the Darkness growing within her nature, demonstrated not least by her interest in blood magic, which had been attempted by Dark mages past. It was

80

more powerful but had proven impossible to stabilise. It had been banned by both White and Red mages, but the Black robes would never agree to anything that stood between a mage and power. Even between the other two orders, there was disagreement. For the White robes, it was a banned subject, while for the Red robes, there was no such thing as forbidden knowledge. So, while Xarnas could not demonstrate any aspect of blood magic, he would not withhold information, so he shared what he knew. Being aligned with the Balance, Dreya's Darkness neither feared nor worried Xarnas, for both Light and Dark magic had a place in the world.

Still, he was curious about Dreya's attitude towards it and so, one day, he came right out and asked her, "Why have you chosen to study and train as a Red robe instead of the Black?"

"You learn more this way," she answered, "gaining control and discipline. Pulling from both sides of the spectrum while being beholden to neither. One day, perhaps, I may take on the Black robes, but I will do so at a time of my own choosing. Dark magic will serve me, not the other way around. That is the mistake Dark mages always make in the end – they lose control. I will not. I shall be mistress of my own destiny, dancing to no-one's tune but my own. I know I am only at the beginning of my journey, but one day, I will be the Greatest Mage Who Ever Lived."

Xarnas did not doubt that at all. At this stage in her training, of course, he had any number of spells up his sleeve that Dreya could not counter and in a mock battle, there were any number of ways he could beat her, although that number was getting smaller almost daily. One thing he could not do, however, was break her control: not of herself and not of her magic. He agreed with her mature assessment of Dark mages: they did lose control until the power consumed them. If Dreya could truly break free of that fate, then her potential was virtually limitless.

I wonder, gentle reader, if Xarnas ever truly realised how far Aunt Dreya would go, just as I wonder if any of us now understand how far she may yet climb.

Dreya's studies with Xarnas lasted a little under five years. She absorbed everything she was exposed to until one day, after a full twenty-four hours of tests, both practical and theoretical, followed by an intense mock battle, the master found that his student had finally surpassed him.

Picking himself up off the floor, where Dreya's magic had left him, he told her, "Congratulations, Dreya. I have taught you all that I can. I have nothing left to give you."

"In that case, Master Xarnas," she said, in that calm, quiet voice of hers, "I see no reason for me to stay any longer. Thank you. You may now retire."

With that, she gathered her red robes around herself and made to leave.

"Where will you go?" Xarnas called after her.

She did not turn around, but she did pause at the door to answer, "Oh, I have a destination in mind. I've known since before I came to you. Now I am ready."

Then, without so much as a 'farewell,' she was gone.

Chapter 13

The Black Tower was situated in its own grounds on the border between the human port town of Gaggleswick, and Ainderbury – a province of the lands of the Faery known as Sylfrania. More than three hundred years ago, it had been the home of the infamous Black wizard, Ulvarius. Widely regarded as the most powerful and dangerous renegade in history, he terrorised the continent, humans and Faery alike, routinely abducting innocent people and subjecting them to the most horrific and torturous of magical experiments. Vast, powerful forces of might and magic assailed him, but he brushed them aside. His power consumed vast acres of land, burning whole towns if but one person defied his will.

It is even said, gentle reader, that Lake Quernhow was formed when a baby dared to cry in the middle of Ulvarius' speech to the people of a town that existed there in his time. In response, he used his magic to make *everybody* cry.

Now, that may not sound so bad, but let me clarify: every human and Faery, every adult and child, every animal and plant within the boundaries of that town cried. Water poured out of every living creature until they were nothing but dried up husks and the ground sank under the weight of the water, forming the lake.

Whether that story is true or exaggerated, I can't be sure. It's another Temporal Black Spot, off-limits to even observation-only Time travel. Good thing, too, for if the legend is accurate, and I bore witness to it, then I fear that I too would cry and never stop. Except perhaps to tear apart the fabric of reality to stop the bastard that did it, plunging the universe into the maelstrom of chaos.

By the end of his time, Ulvarius' influence had expanded until he had virtually the whole of Elvaria in his grasp, and it was only a matter of time before he conquered the world. That is, until one day he did the world a favour and took his own life by jumping off the roof of his tower. No-one knew – or cared – exactly why. Perhaps he was simply consumed by his own power, going the way of so many powerful Dark mages before and since. But there was another legend that said he had learned a prophecy saying that no matter how powerful he became, there would be one other, yet to be born, who would be more powerful still. That brought him both figuratively and literally to the edge, or so the story went.

Whatever the truth of it, in the process of taking his own life, even as he fell, he cast out his magic, cursing the tower and its land. All life within his grounds became twisted under his power, forming devastating defences against any future intruder and casting the Tower under a thick blanket of darkness that had never once abated in more than three centuries since.

Adventurers and knights, wizards and clerics tried to enter the grounds over the years, but none got very far before they were struck down and killed, or worse: absorbed into the very defences that had defeated them.

*****

The red-robed figure materialised in the centre of the town of Gaggleswick, teleporting from Xarnas' home, and gazed at the Black Tower in the distance. It was an impressive, imposing sight. Enshrouded in her hood, Dreya breathed deeply and allowed herself a small smile at the sweet caress of magic all around her. All the power at her command, under her control.

She began to walk, unhurriedly, along the streets of the town, pausing along the way to buy a juicy red apple from a stall along the way. Eating it calmly, she threw away the core just as she reached the gate. Typically, people stayed well away from the border of the Black Tower's gardens of torture, so the sight of this lone red-robed young woman heading for it with purpose and intent attracted a good deal of attention. Many called out to her, warning her, even begging her to go no further, not to throw her life away.

Her only response was, "If I die, I die in the magic. Magic is all."

Taking one more breath, she opened the gate and entered the grounds.

Immediately, she was assailed by spells of fire, ice and lightning, but they bounced harmlessly off her shields. She was sprayed with poison and disease, but none of it could touch her. Animated skeletal warriors attacked her by the dozen, but they were soon dust beneath her feet as she walked. Her pace never wavered, as she encountered animated corpses containing the twisted, tortured souls of former champions who had tried and failed to approach the Black Tower. They

84

wanted to drain her of life and magic, but instead, she drained them, restoring whatever power she had so far expended, freeing their souls in the process. And all the time she drew closer to the tower.

Hellhounds beset her with their teeth, werecats with their claws. A single piercing of her skin would mean the end of her life, but she held out a hand, and all cowered, whimpering before her. Demons that had been trapped there for three hundred years, came at her, desperately. Jealous of her sweet life, shining like a beacon, they sought to snuff it out. Half of them she destroyed, while the other half fled back to the lower planes in terror.

Ulvarius had been a master of the True Undead, in his day. Autonomous creatures with sufficient intelligence to follow complex instructions, yet still enslaved to their creator's will and equiped with regenerative magic. Those that still guarded his tower were the most powerful ever created. Rather than waste her energy trying to kill them – most likely impossible without the use of Holy Water – she focussed her power on the control magic and wrested it from the long-deceased tyrant. From now on, they would serve her, instead.

None of Ulvarius' defences could stop her or even slow her down until, finally, she reached the steps leading to the door of the tower itself. The ragged remains of a robe of black fluttered in the breeze, revealing the bones beneath it: the cursed, skeletal remains of Ulvarius himself. Remains that, the moment Dreya put one foot on the lowest step, picked themselves up off the railings, took on shadowy flesh, wrapped in that tattered old robe and drew itself up to a height of seven feet, looming over Dreya in the form of a lich.

A sibilant voice in Dreya's mind said, '*Long have I waited for thee. Faery blood, no less. Excellent! You see, Ulvarius planned this all along: Ulvarius achieved much before, but that shall be as nothing to what I can do with thy power and mine combined. Thy body and thy magic shall serve Ulvarius for a very long time to come. Now, kneel before Ulvarius and submit thyself!*'

The horrific sound of the lich's laughter carried for miles around. Dreya's hood fell from her head, seemingly blown back by the power of the lich, and the wind its laughter created.

Dreya sank slowly to one knee…

…and casually picked a single black rose, bringing it up to her face to smell, deeply.

Standing once more, she said, calmly, "Get out of my head, go to hell and take your pretentious speech with you. Referring to yourself in the third person is impressing no-one.

"Now is the time!" she declared. "I choose the Darkness."

Her red robes Darkened and lost their colour until they were the deepest, darkest black. Her Realignment complete, Dreya pricked her finger on one of the thorns on the rose's stem. Watching her blood trickle down her hand, she allowed her magic to mingle with it and flow through her veins.

"You are weak, Ulvarius. This is now my home, and you have no place in it."

The lich had now stopped gloating and begun to back away.

'Blood magic? That's impossible!'

Ignoring him, wasting no words, Dreya cast out a beam of dark energy, slamming into the lich, who began to disintegrate before her eyes.

'But blood magic is unstable!' it cried, even as it faded.

"It is perfectly stable," Dreya countered, still never raising her voice. "It just...requires..." The lich exploded and vanished into nothingness, banished to the depths of hell. "...control," Dreya concluded.

With nothing left to impede her, she climbed the remaining steps, opened the door with a look and stepped inside her new home.

*****

Over the next few days, Dreya was seen strolling through her grounds, re-examining Ulvarius' defences, either changing them to better suit her, to ward and protect rather than maim and kill, or eradicating them. She even set the undead guards to work on tidying the gardens. The once perpetual dark sky was banished, giving way to a blazing sun amid high, fluffy clouds and Tempestria's typical swirling vortex of energy.

Most of the people of Gaggleswick adapted, as people often do, and seeing no immediate danger, they continued with their lives, regardless. Once they learned the name of the new Mistress of the Black Tower, a nickname began to surface. When it reached the ears of the sorceress herself, she decided that, while not particularly imaginative, it did have a certain ring to it, and she found she rather liked it. From that day forward, then, it became her official name: Dreya the Dark.

However, the Squire and local assembly were not so content. They all knew the history of the Black Tower and Ulvarius' reign of terror, and they feared that with this new occupant, the violence, horror and bloodshed might begin all over again. The squire filed an objection with the Council of Wizards, but his complaint was thrown out.

He received a reply:

Dear Sir,
Further to your complaint against Dreya the Dark, Black robe sorceress currently occupying the Black Tower.
After due consideration, we write to inform you that the Council of Wizards has ruled in her favour. She has broken no laws of magic, and as such, we cannot countenance any action against her. As for her claim of ownership of said Black Tower, the only former owner of the tower, Ulvarius, has been declared officially deceased for three centuries, so Dreya has merely chosen to make use of a vacant property. Border disputes are generally outside our jurisdiction; however, our research suggests the Black Tower was never officially part of the town of Gaggleswick, being instead its own private estate.
Therefore, on the matter of your complaint, we find there is no case to answer.
Yours in magic,
Laethyn, Justaria, Maia,
Council representatives.

*****

Given this ruling, the Gaggleswick Assembly resigned themselves to their new neighbour, but Squire Johanssen himself was not so easily swayed. He sent an envoy to the ruler of the neighbouring Faery Kingdom of Sylfrania, King Theodorus, to seek his views on the matter. Again, most Faery were inclined to let things be. A Balance aligned Faery wizard had been a curiosity; a Dark aligned one was a scandal, but no-one was interested in doing anything more than gossip about it.

Except for one.

The King's youngest son, Prince Travarin of Ainderbury, the closest Sylfranian province to the Black Tower, was incensed by the ruling. He believed a Dark-aligned Faery was an affront to all that was good, and that Dreya the Dark was already having a corrupting influence on the purity of his daughter, Princess Zarinda, who seemed fascinated by her. The two leaders, then, agreed to launch an attack, before Dreya, having removed most of Ulvarius' defences, had time to build her own.

*****

Three days later, a quad of the bravest holy Knights from Gaggleswick and a trio of the most devout White clerics from Ainderbury entered Dreya's lands, intent on wiping out this dark stain on their community. To their surprise, no magic assailed them, no hellhounds tried to bite them, and the only things the undead warriors were interested in attacking were the weeds. It seemed to these righteous defenders that Dreya had made a grave mistake in leaving herself unguarded. They finally reached the Tower itself, where Dreya the Dark was sitting quietly in the sun, reading a book and sipping a glass of wine. As their shadows fell over her, she finally looked up.

"Greetings," she offered, pleasantly, "and what brings you to my door on such a fine afternoon?"

"Surrender or die, Black Witch!" the knight leader declared.

"'Black Witch' is it, now?" Dreya remarked with raised eyebrows. "And I was just getting used to 'Dreya the Dark.' I do wish you'd make up your minds about my nickname, it's getting hard to keep track."

"Your tower is a blight on the land!" insisted one of the clerics.

Dreya looked hurt as she glanced around her grounds.

"Well, I agree it's a bit of a mess right now, but 'blight' is a bit harsh," she pouted. "Be fair, this mess is three hundred years in the making, and I've been here about three days. I've got my best people working on it."

"You are the scourge of the people, and you must die!" another knight declared.

"Or surrender," Dreya suggested. "At least according to your friend here."

The knight blinked, confused. He had expected a fight, not a debate.

"Well, yes, I suppose you can surrender instead. Do you wish to surrender?"

"Well..." Dreya closed her book and considered the question. "...I'd say that rather depends on what happens *after* I surrender."

The knight leader answered, "You will be taken to Gaggleswick, where you will be tried, sentenced and executed."

Dreya slowly stood. "On what charge?" she asked. "I believe I am entitled to know that, am I not?"

"You are a threat!" said the cleric spokesman, as if it were obvious.

"I'm sorry," said a puzzled Dreya, "who exactly have I threatened?"

"That's for the court to decide," a knight asserted.

"But according to you, the court has *already* decided, since I am to be tried, sentenced and executed. So, it seems to me as if you are giving me a choice between dying here or dying in the town square. That's not much of a choice, is it?"

"Well, it's the only one you're getting!" the lead cleric insisted.

"In that case," Dreya's voice gained an edge of steel and her gaze sharpened to match. "Let me give *you* a choice: leave my lands and never return or enter my service and never leave."

"We will not leave until you die!" the knight insisted; the others murmured their agreement. All readied weapons.

"Very well, I accept your choice," Dreya replied.

With that, she unleashed her power at her enemies. She tore out the knights' souls and discarded them, turning all four into her very own death knight bodyguards, each with the strength of ten mortal knights, unyielding, untiring. Meanwhile, with the clerics, she took the opposite approach. Discarding their lifeless bodies and corrupting their souls, so they became ghouls, floating on the breeze as insubstantial as light and sparking with the power of the gods of Darkness, each one more than a match for any dozen mortal clerics.

"Tell me," Dreya said, "whom do you serve?"

"We serve our Mistress, Dreya the Dark," they chorused.

"And when will you leave my service?" she asked.

"We will not leave until you die," they said.

"Excellent," Dreya approved.

*****

You see, gentle reader? Aunt Dreya gave them a choice – a far better one than the non-choice they gave her – and she accepted their decision. They would serve and protect her, and never leave until the day she died, and technically, gentle reader, a thousand years later, she still hasn't.

Chapter 14

Dreya assigned duties to her attackers, treating them as her household staff, while she retired to her study.

An hour or so later, she emerged with a pair of sealed letters and handed one to each of her two groups with instructions to deliver them to the individuals who sent them to kill her. They were under strict orders to take no hostile action except to defend themselves and ensure the letters reached their recipients on the stroke of midnight. They bowed and obeyed.

That night, Squire Johanssen and Prince Travarin were both shocked to receive their unexpected visitors. With trembling hands, each opened their identical letters, which read:

Dear sir,

You are cordially invited to attend Mistress Dreya the Dark for a banquet at her private residence, the Black Tower, in precisely 72 hours from the moment you receive this letter. Please arrive promptly at the gates to my grounds by the first stroke of midnight, whereupon your hostess will be delighted to escort you to her tower. (Formalwear required, leave all weapons behind, no plus ones.)

Once here, it shall be my honour and privilege to treat you to an evening of delicious food, fine wine and the charming conversation of yours truly.

Then afterwards, we shall retire to my drawing room where we will discuss, in most pleasant surroundings, our future as neighbours in these lands.

At the end of what is sure to be a night to remember, you will, of course, be free to return home to your lives, as usual, all of us secure in the knowledge that there will be no further misunderstandings between us.

Attendance is not compulsory, but it is in your best interests, for should you choose to decline my formal invitation, you will find my terms are not nearly as favourable.

Yours in magic,
Dreya the Dark
Mistress of the Black Tower

p.s. In the interests of safety, please do not attempt to enter my grounds unescorted. A few of the late Ulvarius' defences are having some difficulty adapting to the new regime here, and I would hate for there to be any unfortunate accidents.

Too terrified to do other than as they were told, seventy-two hours later, Squire Johanssen and Prince Travarin were waiting restlessly at the gate to the Black Tower's grounds. On the stroke of midnight, Dreya emerged silently from out of the Darkness. Neither human nor Faery could say whether she had teleported just that second or whether she had been there, unnoticed, as one with the shadows, since before they arrived.

"Good evening, gentlemen," came Dreya's voice from the depths of her hood. "I am so pleased you were able to attend. I trust you had a pleasant journey here?"

Both men nervously agreed that yes, their journeys were indeed trouble-free.

"Excellent," Dreya declared. "Now, if you would allow me…?"

She moved between them, a hand on each one's arm as they strolled through her garden. As they walked, she pointed out various items of interest along the way, and both men were sure to make appropriate appreciative noises.

"Are you two quite alright?" Dreya asked innocently. "You seem almost nervous about something."

Both men scoffed at such an absurd notion. Of course they weren't nervous. Why would they be?

"Why indeed?" Dreya agreed as they reached the steps of her Tower. "It would be extraordinary if you were nervous. After all, you were bold enough when you were sending others into my grounds to attack me, so why would two such brave men be nervous at the prospect of meeting me yourselves, for a harmless little dinner party?"

Before either could think of any kind of response, she removed her hands from their arms and dropped to one knee to examine the black roses. "Look at these!" she exclaimed delightedly. "Aren't they beautiful?"

Both men grabbed this new line of conversation with both hands, waxing lyrical on the astounding beauty of the flowers.

Dreya picked one and stood, turning to face them. "I used one of these roses to banish the lich form of Ulvarius that had been guarding this place for three centuries. Naturally, I know the stories of that time. It must have been terrible to live in the shadow of such a tyrant, not knowing from one moment to the next whether one might live or die at their slightest whim. When it came down to it, though, all I had to do was prick my finger on a thorn." She demonstrated, holding her hand close to their faces so they could watch a trickle of blood run down her fingers and drip onto the ground. "Then I invoked blood magic and he simply vanished in a puff of smoke." She made the rose turn to dust in her hand and blew it in their faces. "Oh, I do apologise," she gasped. "Must have been a freak gust of wind."

As the two men followed her inside, they assured her that there was no harm done and not to worry about such little accidents.

"It's good of you to be so forgiving," she said as two death knight guards opened the doors into the dining hall. There, a ghoul awaited them, carrying, of all things, a white towel as if it were a waiter at a restaurant, there to greet them and show them to their table. Which, of course, was precisely its function that night.

Dreya removed her hood and regarded the two men with a puzzled expression, cocking her head to one side.

"There's definitely something about you two tonight. Are you sure you're not nervous about something?"

Both men assured her they were fine.

"Well, if you're sure. But I should tell you, this is my first time entertaining two such important visitors, so if I say or do anything tonight that makes you the slightest bit uncomfortable, you will tell me, won't you?"

They both agreed they would.

"Promise?" she pressed them.

Forcing a smile, they both promised.

"Excellent," she declared, "now if you would care to follow my ghoulish waiter here, he will show you to your places on the dinner table." She rolled her eyes. "Sorry, slip of the tongue, I meant *at* the dinner table, of course, not *on* it! I mean, it's not like I'm going to gobble you up or anything, is it?" she laughed.

The two men nervously joined in her laughter as they walked into the dining room and stood at their places until Dreya, at the head of the table, sat down.

"Ah, such gentlemen," she said. "Waiting for a lady to sit first."

The ghoul flew away and returned with the wine list.

"Do you mind if I choose?" Dreya asked her guests.

They assured her they didn't mind at all.

"Excellent. Hmmm…Red for tonight, I think," Dreya mused. Let me see…she stabbed the list with a finger. The ghoul flew away again and returned a moment later with a bottle, which he presented to his mistress. When he poured a small amount into a glass for her, she stared at it for a moment, her eyes wide. Dipping her little fingertip into the liquid, she hesitantly tasted a drop on the tip of her tongue. Screwing up her face in disgust, Dreya flushed with embarrassment, and shooed the ghoul away with the bottle and glass. "Don't bother with the list again!" she called after him. "Any will do. Just make sure it's actually wine, this time, and not…blood!"

To her two guests, she said, "I'm so sorry. He's new – I'm just training him up. Only been with me a few days, but then you knew that."

After that, the rest of the dinner passed without incident. They talked about small, inconsequential things and the two men almost started to relax. Almost.

The dinner came to an end and true to her word, Dreya invited them into her drawing room, leaving her 'household staff' to clear everything away.

Settling into soft leather chairs, surrounded by books on shelves, paintings on the walls and a large plush rug on the floor, Dreya took a sip of wine, and remarked, "Isn't this civilised?"

Yes, it was, they agreed.

"Well, think how much more enjoyable it could have been, had you not sent your people to kill me. If you had simply asked to meet me to discuss your concerns, we could have avoided so much unpleasantness. Instead, we are here, as I said in my letter, to discuss our future relations. Specifically, the terms of your surrender."

"Surrender?" the men demanded.

"Of course," Dreya said as if it should be obvious. "You went to war with me, and you lost. Now you have a choice: you can either escalate the conflict, or you can surrender.

"Let me be clear, gentlemen: I am not Ulvarius. Just because a person lives in a house that once belonged to a monster, that does not mean they must be a monster, too. I have no interest in a war with you. I don't do random violence. What I will do is neutralise, without mercy, any threat to my life. I have no interest in your politics. I have no interest in conquest or in ruling the world. If I wanted the world, I could have it tomorrow, but frankly, I wouldn't want the paperwork. Leave me alone to study my magic, and I have no reason to harm any of your citizens."

"So, what exactly are your terms of our…surrender?" Prince Travarin asked hesitantly.

"Well, since you came as requested today, they're straightforward: Leave me alone, and I'll leave you alone. In your case, I am unlikely to venture into Sylfranian lands because it would be…painful for me," Dreya admitted.

There were wards in place, set by White clerics, that would react badly to the presence of her Dark wizard magic.

With a flash of her eyes, however, she warned him, "but don't imagine that would stop me if ever you gave me cause." Point made, she reverted to her usual pleasant, conversational tone. "I would, however, ask for a gift. You know the house and family I belong to, don't you?"

"Of course," he concurred.

"Then I want my ring back, please. You see, I left in something of a hurry and left it behind. Get it for me within seven days, and I guarantee the safety of any messenger carrying it. Can you arrange that?"

The truth was, she didn't care about her ring, and the noble Sylfranian house it represented meant nothing to her, but it meant everything to Travarin.

Working hard to mask how painful it was for him, the Prince agreed to her terms, so Dreya turned her attention to Squire Johanssen.

"The terms for you are slightly different," she said, "because I am very much interested in visiting your town.

"There are bound to be things that I need, so I expect to be granted the freedom of Gaggleswick and full access to its services, just like anyone else. I will, of course, pay the going rate. I always pay my debts. However, as an apology for your thoughtless attack, I would like a gift from you, too. These linen robes of mine are not the most comfortable. They chafe and scratch in places – it's very distracting. Therefore, I would like a bolt of black fabric, please – I'm thinking the softest, most luxurious velvet money can buy – and to hire the services of your finest tailor to ensure a perfect fit every time. Once again, the safety of that tailor will be guaranteed on the condition of absolute discretion on their part."

Without any further explanation for that condition, Dreya concluded, "Now, considering you tried to take my life from me, I consider that a bargain price."

The squire quickly agreed to organise the tailor and have Freedom of Gaggleswick documents drawn up and signed.

"Good. Again, shall we say seven days?"

He assured Dreya that would be no problem.

"Excellent," she said, satisfied. "In that case, gentlemen, our business is at an end." She stood and began to escort them from her home. "I hope you have enjoyed this evening. Do not expect it to happen again.

"One last thing," she added as they reached her door. "You attacked me, yet you still live. Understand the rarity of that. From this day forward, you live only because I choose it. Do not give me reason to choose otherwise. Farewell, gentlemen, and don't worry about walking through my grounds alone. They're all under control now," she assured them.

"Mostly," she added as she closed the door behind them.

*****

After that, gentle reader, she was indeed left alone, and all was well, apart from one incident a few months later, when a mob of hot-headed thugs decided if they couldn't attack Dreya directly, they would go after the one who trained her. After all, it was his fault she was there at all.

Xarnas was a skilled wizard, but it had been a while since he had been involved in a real fight and he was getting slightly worried about the large gang that was advancing on him. He need not have feared, however, as a figure in velvet robes of the deepest black he had ever seen, materialised beside him.

Dreya made short work of the attacking group, sending out an energy beam that incinerated all but one who had been trying to sneak up behind them. Now he turned to flee, instead.

"What was that?" Xarnas gasped in astonishment. "It almost looked like the cannon thing that those higher planar beings fight with."

Dreya inclined her head in respect. "I see your mind has lost none of its sharpness in my absence," she said, getting remarkably close to a compliment. "It's not that powerful, yet, but give me time."

Watching the fleeing man, she said, "I suppose this is the part where I say, 'Let's leave this one alive so he can warn any others what happens if they attack us.'"

"Actually, I've never seen the point of that," Xarnas replied.

"No," Dreya agreed, snapping the ruffian's neck with a flick of her wrist. "Neither have I."

She turned to Xarnas, pulling the hood from her head. "I'll send a message to Squire Johanssen, get him to spread the word that you're under my protection and an attack on you is an attack on me."

"An act of kindness from a Black robe, Dreya?" he wondered.

"Kindness has nothing to do with it," she insisted, flicking her long dark hair out of her eyes, a look of irritation passing over her usually impassive face. "You helped make me what I am. I owe you, and I always pay my debts."

Without another word, she left her former Master's tower for what would be the last time.

In the years that followed, Dreya got more involved with the Council of Wizards, keen to support anything that promoted order and control in magic as well as its protection. The Black division was well known for its infighting, with its wizards vying for power. That exasperated Dreya, as it stood against her dual desires for order and an increase in the power of magic. But if a threat came her way, she would not hesitate to kill her attacker and drain their magic to increase her own. This fuelled her reputation as someone to be feared. She found that useful and did everything she could to cultivate that reputation. That kind of fear, it seemed, meant other wizards didn't attack her. She wasn't afraid of those attacks, but they wasted her time and energy. Dreya hated that.

In time, she grew to be the second-ranked Black robe wizard, which gave her a loud voice on the Council – necessary for some of the reforms and changes she had in mind – but without the excessive administration of the highest position. Dreya wasn't overly keen on the head of her order, Laethyn, but she was confident she would find a way to gain enough influence over him to serve her purposes. Her opportunity came when she saved him from an assassination attempt.

"An act of kindness from Dreya the Dark?" Laethyn wondered, afterwards, when they were together in his office within the Council building.

"I wish people would stop accusing me of that," Dreya muttered in annoyance. "No, I saved you to demonstrate that I have the power of life and death over you. You live only because it suits me. At the same time, I am showing you that I do not want your job. If I did, it would be mine now, and you would be dead."

"So, what exactly does Dreya the Dark want of me?"

"Most of the time you can keep doing as you wish, but your voice carries a lot of weight on the Council, and there will be times when I want your voice to support my position, to make sure I get things done around here."

"Is that all?"

"No, there's one more thing: Don't pick fights. If you think I'm going to rush by to save your life from something you bring on yourself, think again. The infighting has to stop. Pursue your own agenda as much as you like but do it without weakening Dark magic or any other magic for that matter."

"That's just not how things are done, especially in our order."

Dreya invoked her magic to choke him, slowly, cutting through his defences like they weren't there.

"It is now," she said menacingly. She released him. "Are we in agreement?"

Gasping for breath and rubbing his neck, Laethyn nodded.

"But why are you doing this?" he asked. "I've heard you want to be known as the Greatest Mage Who Ever Lived."

"I do," she affirmed. "But I want that to mean something. Look at it this way," she said. "Suppose I wanted to be the world's greatest mathematician: That doesn't mean I want to live in a world where nobody else can add two and two!

"Don't you see?" she cried, throwing her hands in the air in exasperation. It was a rare show of emotion for her. She was just desperate for one other person to understand what she was trying to achieve. "This is too easy! I could kill you with a single thought, but what's the point?" she demanded. "What do I gain? Your title? Your rank? Your office? They mean nothing to me! Even Ulvarius – Tyrant of Tempestria, Scourge of Elvaria – his grounds, his defences, the lich form of the man himself were dust beneath my feet. Don't get me wrong, I enjoyed claiming his Tower – my home is everything I could wish for, but seriously, Scourge of Elvaria?" Dreya snorted, derisively, collapsing in a chair, breathing heavily – she wasn't used to this. "He might as well be called the Menace of Mrs Miggins' Pie Shop for all the threat he was to me! Tell me honestly, can you think of a single mage anywhere in the world who could at least offer me a challenge?"

"Quite frankly, no," Laethyn admitted, grudgingly.

"Exactly, so clearly I need to look beyond this world."

"Other worlds?" Laethyn said, incredulously. "Do you really believe they exist?"

"An interesting thought," Dreya conceded, "and one worth exploring, but right now I have my mind on higher things."

"Higher things?" Laethyn wondered, then he gasped. "You mean…higher planes?"

"Well, I don't want to go there," she said with a wry smile. "I'm not a tourist, but I do want their power. Moreover, I want this world to stand up to those creatures. They come here and fight their battles and don't care how much damage is done in the process. Aren't you sick of it? Don't you want to do something about it?"

Laethyn snorted. "What? You want to save the world now?"

Dreya jumped to her feet like she'd been bitten. "No, I don't want to save the world!" she cried, giving Laethyn a disgusted look. "Don't be ridiculous."

"Then what?" Laethyn wondered.

"I want to kill Daelen StormTiger."

*****

Dreya had long been envious of the shadow warriors' power, gentle reader, even as she railed against the seemingly indiscriminate way in which they used it.

I know my father himself felt as if he were stuck in a loop. Battle after battle he fought, with always the same result: He was evenly matched against his enemy, but Michael always gave Daelen an edge. Enough to beat back his enemy, but only temporarily. It seemed as if nothing would ever break this cycle, but Daelen did not count on one thing: Tempestria was changing, growing, developing.

Mortal magic was out of its infancy now, gentle reader. By the time of Catriona, Mandalee and Dreya, they had already abandoned crawling in favour of walking. In their different ways, each of them had started to run, and soon, very soon…

…they would learn to fly.

Chapter 15

"I'm flying!" Mandalee cried, laughing in joy and exhilaration.

"See, I told you it would work!" Cat called back from her vantage point, sitting on a cloud.

"Remind me never to doubt you again," the White cleric replied.

"Oh, doubt me all you want," her friend countered, "I do! I just see it as a challenge to do it anyway."

"In that case," Mandalee replied, "remind me to challenge you as often as possible because this is amazing! I... AM... FLYING! Woohoo!"

*****

Technically, gentle reader, Mandalee was not really flying. She was actually sitting on the back of a giant albatross, and *it* was flying, but that's just semantics. As for my mother, 'sitting on a cloud' isn't just a metaphor, though it would be an accurate one. She had been working on her druid magic and realised that if she could change the density enough, it would be possible to walk on air. (Again, not a metaphor.) Cat thought it was a better approach than trying to levitate. Floating around would be so undignified. Of course, she could just change into a red-banded falcon, or a tawny owl, which was another thing she'd recently added to her repertoire, but then she couldn't talk. Sympathic communication had its limitations. The other advantage of being in midair in her natural half-Faery form was that she could bring Pyrah along, whenever she was visiting her half-Faery friend.

To say Pyrah 'wasn't keen' on being stuck in a pocket dimension at Catriona's slightest whim, would be a gross understatement. Not that she was that much happier being in midair. Honestly, Cat wouldn't have believed it possible for anyone to complain so colourfully by sympathic means, but somehow Pyrah managed to get her point across...repeatedly.

My mother's Conclave was a good eighteen months behind her now, and with no more college, after their success in tracking down the real Trickster in Compton, she had decided to join Mandalee full time, demon hunting. Jacob had been sad to see her go, but he had always known he could never tie her down. He wasn't sure anybody ever would. ('Tie her down' is *mostly* a metaphor, although there had been a few occasions...)

*****

Demon hunting proved to be the perfect practical outlet for both young women to push the boundaries of their abilities, and sometimes my mother would come up with one of her ridiculous radical ideas. On this day, she reasoned that Mandalee's special relationship with nature should surely extend beyond animals to birds. And if Mandalee could just befriend one that was large enough then, in effect, she would be able to fly.

Cat learned to adapt her access to her pocket dimension so that it would not be affected by Mandalee's clerical magic, thereby avoiding any more clothing mishaps. She had also learned from her experience of being twice stuck in her friend's traps, cut off from nature and therefore the source of her magic. She was determined never to let that happen again, especially when the solution was so simple: carry nature with her at all times. Since druid magic couldn't create something directly from magic alone, she needed ingredients that she could manipulate. An extra bottle of water gave her access to any water or ice-based spells. A few herbs gave her control of plants, even when there were none around. She had also learned to carry a vial of sand from which to create what she called 'Nature's Mirror,' for cosmetic purposes. To her, carrying a selection of small pebbles, weighing nothing at all, meant she had with her the potential for a boulder, a wall, an entire stone shelter, if necessary.

Perhaps the most important lesson she had learned was that, unlike wizard and clerical magic, for druids, size was unimportant for the most part. The scale of what she wanted to create made no difference. Just like in nature: the movement of a single pebble could start a landslide; a slight shift of snow could cause an avalanche; a single spark could lead to a forest fire.

An ice cube in her drink or a towering wall of ice; a potted plant or a towering tree – it was all the same to her. If Cat could provide the seeds, nature could deliver the garden. For the moment, she was wary of doing too much with fire-based spells, for fear of what she might unleash if her ambition outstripped her control. She also didn't bother with any kind of animal control – that was more Mandalee's field,

101

although it wasn't really control, but rather co-operation. Catriona's interest in animals was mostly confined to shapeshifting into them. Wolf-form was her latest success, excellent for long-range land-based scouting and, if necessary, self-defence. She'd even dabbled with a mole form for burrowing underground. Mandalee couldn't for the life of her imagine why her friend would want to do that.

In between demon hunts, the two young women pushed each other's magical abilities. Mandalee would adapt her demon traps to try and counter Cat's ability to escape, forcing Cat to think up a new way to get out. This helped the cleric adapt her magic again and that in turn, challenged Cat's magical imagination once more. In addition to her magic, Cat pulled her archery skills out of mothballs. Mandalee was highly proficient both in hand-to-hand combat and with long-range weapons. In many ways, her fighting style reminded Cat of her mother, except that as much as her friend seemed to dance on the edge, she never crossed the line into a real battle frenzy. She always kept her head, even when she got very drunk. Long-range, it was a close call who was better, and as with their magic, the competition served to raise both their standards.

Council of Wizards rules allowed a mage to train with a single bladed weapon for defence purposes. Just in case they were ever in a situation where their magic wouldn't work, such as in an anti-magic field. Cat had chosen the bow and arrow, which she still routinely carried in her pocket dimension.

Two things had started to bother my mother about the Council generally and the reason behind that rule specifically. In general, the name – Council of Wizards – had begun to feel pejorative. Druids were supposedly acknowledged by the Council and definitely subject to their laws, and yet still it was called the Council of *Wizards*. Not to mention the fact that many female wizards preferred 'sorceress' which, from a certain point of view, made the name sexist, as well.

As for that specific rule, the concept of an anti-magic field seemed bizarre to Catriona. She tried to explain her thoughts on this to Mandalee one day.

"Surely," she said, "an anti-magic field is itself a form of magic. If magic doesn't work within that field, then how does the field operate?"

Unfortunately, gentle reader, Aunt Mandalee was never much of a one for philosophy – she left that to Shyleen. Nor could she muster much enthusiasm for studying, unlike my mother. Conversely, Cat was no match for Mandalee at close range fighting – it wasn't Catriona's style. But diversity is strength, and it worked well for them. While Mandalee was training her body, Catriona was training her mind. She was still very much focussed on her staff, her Angel and of course *Shifting Stars*. Nor had she forgotten her promise to Mandalee. All of her fields of study were progressing – they were just progressing slowly.

Catriona had managed to get her hands on star charts from before what she had begun to refer to as 'The Day of the Angel' to try and distract herself from the fact that it was also 'The Day of the Monster.' The Monster that killed her parents. She had gained this knowledge from a couple of helpful mages who had an interest in astronomy. The wizard helped because he was afraid she would demolish his home if he didn't. The sorceress simply wanted to exchange one book for another. A rare magical text she had been searching for. If there was one thing Cat was good at, it was sniffing out obscure references, so in this way, she fell into a new career as an information trader. Still, on a couple of occasions, she had needed to demolish the wizard's tower to get what she wanted. She always gave them two chances to co-operate without punitive measures, but on her third visit, she would use any means necessary to keep them out of their home, so she could work her magic without harming them. And she always rebuilt their homes, afterwards.

So far, she'd confirmed that part of one constellation had definitely moved out of shape on 'The Day of the Angel' and another section had done so on at least one occasion described in *Shifting Stars*. She wasn't yet ready to accept a causal relationship between that and her staff, but she was intrigued by the possibility, which spurred her on to solve more of the puzzles that allowed her to unlock another level of the security protecting the tantalising higher planar energy at its core. Not that she was especially interested in the power itself. Her fascination lay in the understanding of what it was, why it was so locked away and what knowledge she might gain not just from the final answer, but from the exploration.

Everything my mother learned, she kept in a journal. Although she always seemed to be quite capable of working on five different puzzles in her head, simultaneously, the very process of writing helped her. Putting pen to paper was something she enjoyed for its own sake.

(Like mother, like daughter!) However, as someone who understood the value of knowledge, Cat had developed her own shorthand, which she never shared with anyone, not even Mandalee, ultimately taking the secret language to her grave. Much of her knowledge she shared, but because no-one could read her journals for themselves, she could be sure to do so on her own terms.

Still, even as Catriona had fun with her friend, there was a sense of frustration bubbling underneath. What she needed was a library. Books and resources all in one place. Ideally, one that had lain untouched for a century or two, so that she could research possible earlier sightings of her staff, her Angel and perhaps more shifting stars. It was a bit of an ask, but there was a solution. She'd thought of it some time ago; she'd just hoped to find another way. Unfortunately, the only other possibility was overseas, and she had not the means to get there. That left her with her original idea and her original problem: there was a wizard in the way. Or rather, a sorceress.

As I've said, gentle reader, that was familiar territory for her by now, but Catriona knew this mage would be unlike any she had faced before. Still, the only other choice was to give up…and that just wasn't an option.

Even from her unfamiliar avian point-of-view, Mandalee could read her friend by now.

"Let's land and talk," she suggested.

Cat nodded and manipulated the air around her to create Windy Steps all the way to the ground, while Mandalee asked her albatross to glide down gently. Once on the ground, the bird flew away but promised to return whenever she called.

"Come on then, Cat," said Mandalee as the pair sat down. "Out with it. You've got another of your ridiculous radical plans, haven't you?"

Cat nodded.

"But this – whatever this is – is different, isn't it?"

"What makes you think so?"

"You're not happy about it."

With a rueful smile, Cat replied, "You're not going to be happy about it, either.

"OK, now I definitely need to know!"

Steeling herself, Catriona took a deep breath and said, "There's only one place I can go, now, that could have what I need for my research. *All* my research. My staff, my Angel, my magic, the stars…" she looked her friend in the eye, "…you."

"And that place is…?" Mandalee prompted.

"The Black Tower," Cat stated, flatly.

"What!" Mandalee gasped. "You can't possibly be serious!"

Cat insisted she was. "I told you, you wouldn't like it!"

"You're planning to go up against Dreya the Dark? There isn't enough alcohol in the world to get me drunk enough to make that sound like a good idea!"

"It's not a good idea," Cat replied. "It's just the only idea."

"OK, let me get this straight. You're going to – what – ask Dreya the Dark very nicely twice, and when she refuses, assuming the sorceress hasn't killed you, you're going to attack her and demolish the Black Tower itself?"

"Don't be ridiculous," Cat shook her head. "I'm not going to attack her; I'm desperate, not suicidal. No, I need to do something far more difficult: I need to impress Dreya the Dark."

Mandalee snorted, "I don't think Dreya the Dark does 'impressed.'"

"That's because she hasn't met me, yet," Cat replied.

"Oh!" Mandalee laughed. "So, because I fell for your charms after you blundered into my traps, you think Dreya's going to do the same?"

Cat offered a mischievous smile. "Are you saying you don't believe I can do it?"

"Message getting through, at last, is it?"

"Is mine?" Cat retorted.

"What do you mean?" Mandalee asked with a frown.

"You're doubting me again, and I've told you how I react when you doubt me."

Mandalee groaned, "You take it as a challenge to do it anyway!"

Catriona stood, confidently. "Challenge accepted!" she declared. "All I need now is your blessing."

Mandalee, too, got to her feet and embraced her friend. "Always," she insisted. "You know that. Whatever ridiculous radical plans you come up with, I have your back, no question."

When they broke the hug, Cat's smile had grown into a broad grin. "Thanks for the support," she said, "but when I said I needed your blessing, I actually meant your clerical blessing. Specifically, on my arrows." She pulled a few clear of her quiver. "And maybe a bottle of water or two."

"What ever for?" Mandalee wondered.

Cat laughed. "Don't worry, Mandalee," she said. "It's all part of my ridiculous radical plan!"

*****

Catriona didn't head straight for Gaggleswick and the Black Tower. First, she had another destination in mind, flying all the way to the home of the Red wizard, Xarnas, who had trained Dreya. Nobody else could know Dreya the Dark half as well as him, and that was information she needed.

My mother had already done background research on Xarnas and discovered a useful little nugget of information. His youngest daughter was married to a Faery boy, and they were expecting their first child. Out of respect for the boy's heritage, Xarnas wanted to give them a special gift: a book of traditional Faery children's rhymes and lullabies. Such a book was tough to find without the right Faery contacts since human-Faery relationships were still something of a rarity at the time.

Even Catriona herself couldn't find a book that was good enough, in her opinion, so pulling from her childhood memory of growing up among the Faery, she had written her own.

Xarnas was astonished by the book when Catriona knocked on his door, introduced herself and presented it to him.

Recognising Catriona's Faery heritage, he told her, "I'd wager that much of what you've written here is deeply personal to you."

Cat felt a pang of regret, thinking about her fantastic childhood and the parents she had lost far too soon.

"Yes, you're right," she nodded, sadly, "but I felt it had to be that personal, to match the value of the information I seek in exchange. In fact, no," she reconsidered, "not 'in exchange.' For once, I'm not going to trade the human way. I'm happy to hear of another human-Faery couple and delighted that a great man such as yourself would respect Faery culture enough to give them such a book. In Faery culture, trade is based on giving freely that which is precious, so in that spirit, the book and all it contains are a gift from me to you, given freely, so that you might, in turn, give it freely to your daughter and son-in-law, and they eventually to their child."

"In that case," Xarnas said, "it seems to me, as a point of honour, that I should give freely to you something that is precious to me. What can I do for you?"

Cat told him she wanted to learn everything she could about Dreya the Dark.

Xarnas studied Catriona as he considered that. "When most people ask about Dreya, they either want to know about her extraordinary power, or how I could train what they see as a 'servant of Darkness.' Some have even been known to use the word 'evil.'" He shrugged. "At least they're honest: many others think it while not daring to say it. I suspect you are not like any of these."

Cat shook her head, emphatically. "I would never be so pejorative," she promised, "and I very much doubt Dreya is a servant of anything."

She explained further that she was not only interested in Dreya's powers and abilities, but also the Faery woman herself. Her personality, her interests – to understand her, or at least begin to.

"A laudable goal," Xarnas approved. "To seek knowledge and understanding lies at the heart of our Red order of Balance."

With that, he invited her into his home, where he was pleased to tell her everything she wanted to know.

He also told her he had heard varying accounts of Catriona Redfletching, but the only one he paid attention to was Justaria, his successor on the Triumvirate, who described her as 'a handful of trouble.'

"I'm certain she intended it as a compliment."

Cat smiled a smile of secrets. "Oh, you have no idea how much trouble I can be," she said, eyes dancing with mischief. "I'm a veritable Trickster, sometimes!"

Xarnas grinned, "And that is exactly what you will need to be to grab Dreya's attention. If you want to impress her, you will have to fight her without ever attacking her."

He paused for a moment, before adding, "I would never tell this to anyone else, no matter what they tried to trade, but in the spirit of giving freely, I will say this: I feel sorry for Dreya the Dark."

Cat was stunned. She never would have imagined hearing such a statement, but now that he'd said it, she knew this was the most critical part of their conversation. This was why she'd come here. More than anything else, this was what she needed to know.

Xarnas explained himself, saying, "She once told me her ambition was to be known as the Greatest Mage Who Ever Lived."

Cat nodded. She could understand that sentiment. She didn't share it – she didn't think of her druid magic in quite those terms – but she could understand it. In many ways, it was admirable: if you're passionate about something, why not strive to be the best?

"But to my mind," Xarnas continued, "that title is hers already. Think about it: You've studied the reign of terror for which Ulvarius was responsible three centuries ago?"

Again, Cat nodded, not wanting to disturb the moment by speaking.

"Well, it's easy to imagine the story of a powerful mage, working their whole lives to try and take his tower, remove the blot on the landscape that he left behind as a deadly, terrifying legacy. Then maybe, after decades of preparation and study, at the peak of their powers, they finally succeed at some terrible personal cost, and retire to their well-earned new home."

Once more, Cat nodded. The story practically wrote itself, and she knew the twist that was coming.

"But Dreya finishes her apprenticeship with me and takes the Black Tower in five minutes flat, with nary a scratch apart from a prick on her finger from a single rose thorn, as she invents stable blood magic practically on the spot."

Cat knew the story – everybody did – she'd just never looked at it the way Xarnas did.

"Then, having moved in and begun to make the formerly dangerous place a thing of beauty, her new neighbours attack her! Attack her? They should have been thanking her! I swear, if she hadn't ripped out their souls, I would have done it myself!"

Catriona placed a gentle, reassuring hand on his arm. He was almost in tears; such was his passion.

"So, what's left for her? She's so young, especially by Faery standards. She's achieved more than any mage in history, and it's not enough."

Catriona understood. "She's bored," she realised. "She must be."

"And that's why I feel sorry for her. Be creative, Catriona, be inventive. Keep her guessing. Don't underestimate how dangerous she is and don't let her pin you down, literally or figuratively. Keep her off balance, never knowing what's coming next, and I truly believe you might just succeed. I hope so, because in my opinion, knowing Dreya as I do, a 'handful of trouble' could be exactly what she needs in her life."

Chapter 16

My mother had learned her lessons well, gentle reader, and by this stage of her life, she refused to go into any situation unprepared. For this action, she knew she had to do her homework like never before. She would get only one shot at this, and if her preparations were anything less than meticulous, she would fail. Perhaps even die.

Thanks to Xarnas, she had done the theory, and her magic was as prepared as it was ever going to be. There was just one more factor to consider: the lay of the land. If she were going to impress Dreya the Dark, she would have to confront her in her own grounds. Typically, of course, the land was a friend to my mother, but these lands were different. They had once belonged to Ulvarius, but Dreya had tamed them and made her own.

It was the night before Midsummer, and under cover of darkness, Cat flew over Sylfrania in the form of a tawny owl. Unsurprisingly, the whole Faery woodlands were in full bloom. Midsummer's Day was a big day of romance in Faery culture and a traditional day for prominent weddings. As a Quarthonian Faery, she wasn't up with Sylfranian politics, but doubtless both communities would be busy tomorrow.

Passing over Ainderbury and crossing into human lands, she found a quiet perch in a tree in Gaggleswick, close to the Black Tower, and took a moment to rest and go over her plan. In this form, she was hopeful that she could scout Dreya's lands with impunity. In truth, she had no way of knowing how far Dreya's powers of detection might extend, but this was the best she could do. She had decided to forgo any red bands, confident that she was too focused on her goal to lose herself. In fact, she was mostly ready to let go of that crutch altogether, except for her red-banded falcon, just because it was the first form she'd successfully used and after so long, it wouldn't feel right without the red bands. Catriona was encouraged when a passing barn owl seemed to take a liking to her. If another owl was convinced of her 'owliness' and did not find anything strange about her, she was hopeful that any detection magic would be equally unconcerned.

Resuming her flight and crossing into Dreya's lands, she could see Xarnas had not exaggerated about the beauty of Dreya's grounds, now that she had had time to work on them. In fact, Cat grudgingly admitted that she couldn't have done much better herself. Dreya had transformed this patch of nature, freeing it from a three-hundred-year curse. It would not easily be turned against her. Catriona had prepared for this, however. That's why she was here.

As I have said previously, gentle reader, my mother routinely carried nature with her, but for this, she needed to go one step further and plant the literal seeds of success in Dreya's grounds.

She had been carrying plant seeds in her beak since she transformed, and now she let them fall onto the ground beneath her. She was glad to spit them out, but it had been the only way. Using her pocket dimension magic here would no doubt set off all kinds of alarm bells, which would be counter-productive, to say the least. As it was, she only had to use a tiny bit of druid magic, in essence, whispering to the soil to move ever so slightly, to cover the seeds, and encouraging them to begin to quietly germinate. Job done, for now, she flew away to get some rest. She would be back in the middle of the day in a different form.

*****

At noon the next day, as the sun beat down upon the Black Tower, a red-banded falcon was perched on a tree just outside the grounds observing, with her sharp eyes, the black-robed woman sitting on the steps of the Tower, reading a book of magic and occasionally sipping on a glass of wine. The bird also observed the patches of greenery that had grown overnight. Plants that wouldn't look at all out of place unless the observer was keenly in tune with nature. Certainly not the undead guards that served as groundskeepers. The stage was set, the player was ready. Time for the performance to begin.

Gliding silently to the ground, Catriona reverted to her natural form, pulling her clothes and spell ingredients out of her pocket dimension, as well as her bow and arrows. She was nervous but embraced the butterflies as she walked calmly but purposefully towards the ornate iron gate that opened into Dreya's gardens.

The groundskeepers paid her no heed. Dreya didn't often entertain visitors, but neither did she kill everyone who set foot on her land. Her guards and defences would react only in the event of a threat to Dreya herself. Cat had to make sure to not play her hand too soon. For now, she had to walk and wait.

After a few minutes, Catriona arrived at the optimum distance from where Dreya sat and, making no sudden movements, came to a natural halt. Tied to the end of her arrows, along with her trademark red fletching, were roses – some red, some white. Being careful of the thorns, she nocked a non-matching pair and let them fly, swiftly followed by another and a third. The half dozen arrows never got close to Dreya, sailing high and wide to stick to her doorframe, thanks to some magically modified tree resin on the flattened tips. From there, the flowers grew into a rosebush that blocked the entrance entirely.

Dreya's groundskeepers stopped their gardening and moved threateningly towards Catriona, but a quick mental word with nature caused the plants she had seeded to proliferate and grab them, the stems wrapping around them and preventing any movement. The more they struggled, the more the plants grew, and the tighter they squeezed.

Unconcerned, Dreya placed a bookmark in her book, closed it and put it away in a pocket in her black velvet robes.

Cat found herself feeling quite envious of Dreya's robes. They looked so soft! Their colour was, without doubt, the blackest black she had ever seen – as if they were spun from the fabric of the night sky. Dreya glanced behind her at the roses and then finally looked up at Catriona.

"That's an original way to deliver flowers," she remarked.

"Oh, I'm nothing if not original," Cat replied.

"And what's the occasion?"

"Occasion?"

"Well, call me old-fashioned, but when someone brings me flowers, there's usually an occasion of some kind."

"Usually?" Cat wondered. "Do people bring you flowers often, then, Dreya?"

"No," Dreya admitted. "Not often. In fact, I can't remember the last time anyone did. Which brings me back to…"

"…an occasion," Cat finished, nodding. "OK, that makes sense. Well, I suppose you could say they're a 'thank you.'"

"A 'thank you'? For what?"

"For agreeing to my proposal."

Dreya arched her perfectly plucked eyebrows. "You're proposing to me now?"

Cat winced slightly at her choice of words and warned herself not to be too smart mouthed. Catriona loved playing with words, but clearly, she was in the presence of a master wordsmith. She'd meant to say 'proposition' but having said 'proposal,' she had little choice but to go with it.

"Well, it is Midsummer's Day," she reminded Dreya. Perhaps that was the reason for her slip of the tongue. "But I think we should take it slow," she said, "date a bit first. Starting with, say, a study date in your library."

"Interesting idea," Dreya remarked, "although if we're going to be dating and eventually married, it seems to me I should probably at least know your name."

"Thought you'd never ask," said Cat. "I'm Catriona Redfletching, and you're going to give me access to your library before this day is done."

Dreya got to her feet with a kind of fluid grace that reminded Catriona of Shyleen when she'd spotted some fascinating prey, just before her claws came out.

"'Before this day is done,' eh?" Dreya echoed. "Someone's been doing her homework, but then Xarnas does like to brag about his finest student. Not that I can blame him."

"Well, you are his crowning achievement."

"Flattery will get you nowhere," Dreya said, dismissively.

"No flattery," Cat assured her. "You're Dreya the Dark – you're famous."

"As are you, Catriona Redfletching," Dreya replied. "According to legend, you're quite happy to demolish a wizard's entire home just to get your hands on a single book. I can only imagine what you'll do for an entire library."

Cat gave her a crooked smile. "I'm showing you what I'm prepared to do."

"Do you really believe you can just tear the Black Tower apart? Do you really think you have that power?"

"Power isn't everything," Cat shrugged, "and what I believe is that I will have access to your library before this day is done."

"And what's to stop me calling on my grounds' defences to kill you where you stand?"

Cat glanced around, making a show of being unconcerned. "Your guards seem to be a bit tied up at the moment."

Dreya snorted, "If you've done this much prep work, you must know I have a lot more defences than that. Unlike Ulvarius, I keep them dormant, because I'm not insecure enough to jump at every shadow that passes across my land." She paused before adding pointedly, "No matter what shape that shadow might take."

Cat fought the urge to respond to that. It was possible Dreya knew all about her avian activities. However, it was equally likely the sorceress knew only that she *could* shapeshift and was simply making a perfectly reasonable guess. Cat was an information trader, and she wasn't going to make the mistake of volunteering information just because the other party *might* already know. She'd used that trick herself.

"Still," Dreya continued, "it only requires a thought to reactivate them, if necessary. So, tell me, Catriona Redfletching—"

"—Call me Cat," she interrupted, taking back some control over the conversation.

"Very well, Cat it is, then, and while we're on the subject of names, given my rank as Secondmage of the Black order, you really should address me as *Mistress* Dreya, according to Council rules."

"Actually, I have a few issues with Council rules," Cat told her.

"So do I," said Dreya.

"You see? We've got something in common. Our date's going really well already!"

"It is, isn't it?"

"Sorry," Cat apologised. "You were going to ask me something and I interrupted you."

She was determined not to let the supreme mistress of control have things her own way, so she made it seem as if Dreya needed her permission to continue.

"That's OK," Dreya accepted, showing not a hint of irritation. "I was just talking about my defences."

"What about them?"

"Well, why shouldn't I activate them and be rid of you?"

Cat pounced. Now she knew she'd got Dreya's attention.

"Because you're not insecure enough to jump at every shadow that passes across your land," she said. "Come on, Dreya, if you want to be rid of me, do your own dirty work!"

"An excellent suggestion," Dreya conceded. "I could use the exercise."

Without warning, she conjured a flight of poisoned darts that flew towards Catriona, but a sudden gust of wind blew them harmlessly away.

"OK, direct approach, then," Dreya remarked, focussing her magic to create the poison directly from the magic inside Catriona's body.

Cat shot her a withering look. "Really, Dreya? Poison? I'm a druid – we're awesome at curing poisons."

"Well then, let's see how you fair if I take your magic away."

Dreya had developed the ability to literally drain magical power from a wizard's body, take it for herself. But Cat wasn't a wizard, she was a druid. Her magic came from an entirely different source.

"You can't drain me because the power isn't really mine. It's the power of nature herself, and you can't drain nature." Some of Catriona's plants began to extend themselves towards the sorceress. "Come on, Dreya," she said. "Take me seriously, or I'll just tie you up in your garden and demolish your tower, after all!"

"Alright then," Dreya agreed. "Let me take things up a notch." With that, she unleashed flames from her fingertips, but Cat threw some water in the air and directed it to form a jet of water in the path of the flaming attack, extinguishing it, harmlessly. Dreya upped the power to a pair of fist-sized fireballs, but Cat used more water to create a suspended aquatic shield that blocked the strike.

"So, you need water to make water," Dreya observed. "What happens if you run out?"

She invoked her magic, and Cat's water bottles shattered, spilling their contents on the ground. Then, for good measure, she caused the spilt water to boil away, robbing Cat of her aquatic resources...or so she thought.

"Well?" she prompted. "Where are you going to get your water from now?"

"Dreya!" Cat admonished her. "I thought you'd be more observant than this. Haven't you noticed the sun?"

Dreya glanced up at the sky.

"It's gone behind some clouds, so what?"

"Look at those clouds, Dreya," Cat said. "Really look. Clouds like that mean only one thing. It looks to me like it's going to..."

Right on cue, the rain began to pour – hard!

"Well, you certainly have a flair for the dramatic," Dreya remarked, approvingly. "Just two questions: First, if you can make it rain on cue, why carry water around with you?"

"Partly for convenience, but mostly because the rain makes my hair go frizzy."

For the first time, there was a flicker of something on Dreya's face, and while Cat wouldn't go so far as to call it a smile, it was a beginning.

"Second question?" she prompted.

An enormous fireball, three feet in diameter grew between Dreya's hands. "Do you think a bit of rain is enough to stop this?"

In response, the rain in the air between them became a waterfall, a curtain of water separating them.

"This might," said Cat.

Dreya just shook her head, sending the fireball forth. Cat was confident of her aquatic shield, but to her surprise, instead of passing *through* it, the fireball quickly darted *around* it. Choosing the better part of valour, Cat shifted to her falcon form and tried to fly away from the approaching fireball, calling off the rain to make flying more comfortable, but no matter what aerobatics she tried, it tracked her every move. She'd never tried to use weather control magic in another form before, but staying as a falcon was the only way she could stay ahead of the fire. It helped that it was the first form she'd ever mastered. By now, it was almost as familiar to her as her real body, which meant she didn't need much concentration to maintain it. Compartmentalising what her avian-self needed, she devoted the rest of her brain to manipulating the airflow around the moving fireball into a mini-whirlwind, spinning faster and faster until it removed the air from the eye and extinguished the flames.

That done, she shifted back to her true self in midair, standing on one of her Windy Steps.

"Didn't your mother ever tell you not to play with fire?" she wondered.

"I think she may have said something about that," Dreya admitted, "but then she also told me to marry a prince, who was willing to overlook certain things, and get showered with rose petals in a traditional marriage ceremony. As if becoming a Faery princess should have been the pinnacle of my ambitions." She shrugged. "I tended not to listen to my mother too much after that."

Catriona flattered herself that if Dreya the Dark was volunteering personal information now, then she was definitely making an impression.

"Still," Dreya continued, "perhaps you're right. Maybe I should change things up now. Let's see how you handle this!"

Cat felt the tiny hairs on her arms start to stand up in response to the build-up of charge around the sorceress that was clearly going to develop into a lightning bolt heading in her direction. The druidess had just the thing. Out of her pocket dimension, she pulled out, of all things, a bucket of water, which she threw all over Dreya the instant the bolt was ready, causing it to backfire, painfully. While the sorceress was momentarily stunned, the druid used that same water to trap Dreya in a cylindrical cage of ice.

"Don't play with electricity, either," Cat admonished her, as she stepped back down to the ground. "Especially with so much water around."

Dreya levitated out of the trap, scoffing at Cat leaving such an obvious escape.

"I'm insulted if you think that would be any kind of challenge."

"Back at ya!" she retorted, making the wind pick up so much that Dreya was thrown back down to the ground with a bump. "As if I'd leave such an obvious escape route without it leading to a trap! You're still not taking me seriously, Dreya. Stop holding back – show me what you've really got, or I might start to doubt that you're really as powerful and deadly as you make out."

"Alright," Dreya acceded. "If you're sure that's how you really want it. Just remember you asked for it!"

With that, for the next half hour, Dreya turned up the power and frequency of attacks, putting Cat firmly on the defensive, working frantically to counter whatever came her way. Cat kept on the move, never letting Dreya pin her down, countering with magic or shapeshifting to escape and buy time. The way she ran up and down her Windy Steps, Cat was thankful that her time with Mandalee had got her in shape. Still, she needed a breather for a minute and decided to put a barrier between them while she got her breath back. Throwing a few pebbles on the ground, she grew a stone wall between them as she landed. She didn't think Dreya would try to levitate over it after what happened the last time. Hopefully, breaking through it would at least take a minute.

"Stonewalling me now, Cat?" Dreya called out. "And here was me thinking we were communicating really well since we started dating!"

"Oh, you know how it is," Cat returned. "Everybody in a relationship needs their own space, sometimes!"

"True," Dreya allowed, invoking her magic to shatter the stone into fragments, "but I'm all about breaking down barriers and moving forward. Standing still for too long can be bad for you. It can take the magic right out of a relationship."

Cat found herself suddenly surrounded by an anti-magic field. "But our two magics are different," Cat pointed out.

"Yes, of course, I know you're a druid – don't think I haven't adapted the field to take that into account."

"You know, I really don't get these things," Catriona said. "An anti-magic field is itself a form of magic, so how does it operate?"

"It works on a different frequency to other magic and cuts off all other frequencies but its own."

"Interesting," said Cat, "so in theory, if I could determine the right frequency, I could adapt my magic to run off the field itself."

Dreya's eyes widened slightly, betraying interest in a concept she hadn't considered before.

"Can you do that?"

"Not yet," Cat admitted, to Dreya's apparent disappointment, "but you've just given me a big piece of the puzzle. Give me time."

"Time's something you don't have. You're trapped."

Cat shook her head. "I've been in worse traps than this, and after criticising me for leaving an obvious escape route, earlier, you've done the same thing."

Dreya scoffed, "I don't make mistakes like that – the field forms a dome over your head. You can't fly out."

"Wasn't planning to," Cat returned.

The anti-magic field only blocked her from sending her magic outside the barrier, she could still use it on herself, so she shifted to her mole form and burrowed underneath. While she remained underground, Dreya had no way to track her until she came back up and nipped Dreya on the ankle. As the sorceress whirled around, Cat shifted straight to falcon form and flew up into the air over Dreya's head, where she reverted to her true self and stood on her Windy Steps.

"If this were a real battle," she said, "I'd have changed to wolf form and bitten you properly, or falcon form and pecked out your eyes, or owl form and...hooted...really loud...or something."

Dreya's face twitched to a half-smile, just for a moment before she could get it under control. "Started well, that threat."

"Wasn't trying to threaten you; I was trying to make you laugh. Almost succeeded, too!"

"You're not that funny," Dreya refuted.

"I am so that funny!" Cat insisted. "Come on, this one was a classic!" she said, pulling another bucket out of her pocket dimension, brandishing it over Dreya's head.

"Using the same trick twice, Cat? I'm disappointed."

"Dreya!" Cat rebuked her. "As if I would!"

Cat tipped the bucket's contents over Dreya, but it wasn't water, this time, but rose petals.

Chapter 17

"What the—?" Dreya began, unsure how to react to the flurry of rose petals fluttering around her in the breeze. Given the way druid magic worked, it was entirely conceivable that this might be some new, inventive form of attack, although Dreya couldn't imagine what offensive use rose petals could have.

"Well, I thought our relationship was going so well," Cat explained, "we could skip right to the wedding." Then with a mock hurt look, she asked, "I didn't misread the situation, did I?"

This time Dreya's smile was fuller and lasted longer. "I think it's a bit too soon, that's all. I haven't accepted your proposal yet."

"Ah, but you're going to. You're almost there, I can tell!"

"You're very sure of yourself," Dreya said, putting on her very best frown.

"Aww, don't be like that – at least let me blow you a kiss!"

The wind picked up, suddenly, forcing Dreya back towards her tower steps. Cat had noticed the rain had left a pool of water at the bottom, which gave her an idea of how to get Dreya to do something she'd planned from the beginning. Unfortunately, she hadn't pushed Dreya quite far enough. Doing the same thing twice would make Dreya suspicious. She needed one more roll of the dice. It was highly dangerous, but it was the only way.

"How was that for you?" Cat quipped, trying to use their verbal sparring to manipulate Dreya.

"Well I must admit, I was very moved, but you're still no nearer getting inside my tower."

"Oh, I'm closer than you realise," Cat retorted, "and if you want to stop me, you'll have to stop playing and fight me properly. "Come on," she demanded, "you didn't fight Ulvarius with these tricks!"

"No, I used blood magic."

"But that's unstable!" Cat mock gasped.

"It's perfectly stable. It just needs control."

"Yes, I've heard you like to be in control, so control me. If you can. Come on, Dreya, turn up the power all the way: show me what you can really do. Show me your famous blood magic. I'm not going to believe you can really do it unless you show me."

"Don't try to goad me – it won't work."

Cat knew that. Dreya's refusal was part of the plan. "Not trying to. I know what you can do. Aren't you curious to know what I can do? Alright, forget blood magic. Best conventional spell. In fact, tell you what, you can blast me with your deadly magical energy beam."

"You know about that?" Dreya wondered. "Oh, of course, I used it to defend Xarnas," she realised. "You can't really want me to do that."

"Yes, I do," Cat insisted, "and I'll fight you with…let's see…" she made a show of checking what spell components she still had left, "…a handful of sand."

"You'll die."

"What do you care?"

"I don't. It's just a shame to end the fun so soon."

Cat pounced on the victory. "Ha! I got you to admit you're having fun!"

Dreya actually winced, conceding the point.

"But seriously," Cat continued, "quite a few wizards will thank you. I've become something of a thorn in their side."

"Like old Renjaf," Dreya said.

It was Cat's turn to be surprised.

"You're not the only one who does their homework," Dreya told her.

"Renjaf will probably send you flowers and have my friend Jacob deliver them," Cat said, recovering quickly. "You can say hi to him for me. Anyway, are we doing this or not?" As she was speaking, she slowly, casually, moved towards the optimum position that she had in her mind.

"It's your funeral. Any special requests for that, by the way?"

"Just bury me here in your garden if you don't mind. I like what you've done with the place."

"Thanks. It's certainly a big improvement on the Black Tower's previous owner's taste. Tell you what: I'll cut down those roses you grew around my door and put them on your grave."

"Sounds nice."

"Well, it's been a whirlwind romance, Cat," Dreya considered. "I only just met you, and yet we've dated, you've proposed, we've got married, and now I have to plan your funeral."

"Ours is a tragic love," Catriona agreed, solemnly, coming to a natural, gentle halt so that she could draw an exact straight line between herself, Dreya and the door to the Black Tower. She wanted the sorceress up those steps. Now in position, she grew the plants around her to grip her tightly in place no matter what Dreya threw at her.

"OK, then," Dreya said. "Ready?"

"Ready," Cat confirmed, fist closed tightly around her sand so it couldn't trickle out.

Without further warning, Dreya built up her power and shot out her energy beam. Cat threw her handful of sand into the air and fused it, turning it instantly into Nature's Mirror, reflecting the energy right back. Dreya shielded as Cat knew she would, but the force of the blast sent her recoiling backwards to sprawl on the steps of her Tower.

Cat silently celebrated. She'd got Dreya the Dark exactly where she wanted her.

Dreya was literally and figuratively stunned. Picking herself up, she demanded to know how Cat had done that.

Cat explained, "Druid magic is the opposite of wizard magic, in a way. I take the power you use, change it, recycle it and send it back. So, logically, if you think about it…"

"…the right kind of druid magic shield can reflect my wizard magic," Dreya concluded. "Excellent." Then with a dangerous gleam in her eyes, she suggested, "Shall we see if it works just as well against blood magic?"

Cat was indignant. "If you're determined to be Miss Serious Face again, I'm going to start getting all frosty, too!"

The pool of water froze at the base of the steps and grew into an ice wall, keeping Dreya trapped on her steps, unable to set foot in her garden, cut off from her black roses.

"Oh, I see what you're doing," Dreya said. "Nice move. Thing is, though, I don't need my black roses for blood magic – not when you've provided roses of your own."

She reached out to prick a finger on the roses around the door, but the rosebush reached out to grab her instead, immobilising her without breaking the skin so as not to give her access to the kind of magic she was trying to unleash. Dreya was in obvious pain.

"My arrows were fashioned from the same wood as those roses," Catriona explained, "and I had them blessed by a White cleric friend of mine who has a particular affinity for nature. Quite painful for a Dark wizard, I imagine."

She grabbed her Crystal Mage Staff out of her pocket dimension – the better to make an imposing impression as she walked close, just behind her ice wall.

"You see, there's a drawback to wizard magic. You need to use your hands to inscribe the language of magic in the air. You can't do magic if you can't move. Now, I'm not sure about blood magic, but I figure if you're immobilised, you can't prick yourself, so you can't access that power!"

Dreya's smile was chilling, and suddenly Cat wasn't quite so smug. Her mind raced, frantically, trying to see if there was something she'd overlooked. If there was, she couldn't see it.

"If you were dealing with any other wizard, you'd be right," Dreya conceded. "But this is me. Do you really think I'd let this stop me? Here's a little thing I've been working on…"

She focussed her gaze on Cat through the clear ice and spoke but one word.

"STUN."

Cat found herself completely unable to move. A new anti-magic field formed around her, skin-tight and completely encasing her from the top of her head to the soles of her feet. Dreya wasn't one to make the same mistake twice.

Dreya moved her penetrating gaze to the roses trapping her.

"BREAK."

The wood and green stems snapped, allowing Dreya to step clear.

"SHATTER," she told the ice wall, and it blew apart into a million fragments.

Cat was grateful that Dreya's stun magic allowed her to close her eyes against any incoming ice shards. She still had her eyes shut tight as she felt Dreya's breath on her face.

"SQUEEZE," came Dreya's voice, and at her command, a force of magic took hold of Cat in a vice-like grip.

Her eyes flew open in genuine fear and panic.

"Shapeshift into something smaller, and I squeeze tighter," Dreya warned her. "Finally out of tricks, druid? Feel free to nod your head."

Cat thought hard but had to admit defeat. She nodded.

Still not releasing her, Dreya turned her attention to Catriona's Crystal Mage Staff. "Interesting staff you've got there. It seems to be giving off higher planar energy as well as a very mixed up magic signature, like druid, wizard and cleric magic all squeezed together like, well, like you are at the moment," she taunted, like a spider savouring her power and control over the annoying insect snared in her web. "Mind if I take a closer look?" Dreya asked. "Oh, that's right, you don't have a choice, do you?"

Higher planar energy was the power of the shadow warriors. The power Daelen StormTiger wielded. If ever she was going to take him on as she planned, she would need that power. She had begun experimenting with the residual traces left behind after their devastating battles. Scraps off the shadow warriors' table. But the power within the staff this druid girl possessed was a feast by comparison. It was irresistible.

Dreya reached out, but as soon as her hand touched the staff, a brilliant flash of energy broke all magical bindings and sent both mages flying. Cat landed in the soft garden. Dreya was not so lucky. Her head collided with her door, throwing it wide open and knocking her unconscious.

This was Catriona's first peek inside the Black Tower. She could see that the front door led to a large porch or portico area, and eventually to an interior door made of frosted glass. Through that glass, Cat could just make out figures rushing closer: Dreya's personal staff, she realised. Presumably, while Dreya was conscious, she had kept them out of it, preventing them from interfering while she 'dealt with' Cat, personally. But with Dreya unconscious, there was nothing holding them back anymore. They were going to come rushing out, believing their Mistress to be under attack.

Catriona had never intended to seriously harm Dreya – throughout their fight, she had carefully avoided that – but her elite guards were not likely to take intentions into account. They would kill Catriona without a moment's hesitation.

Cat still had a couple of small vials of the water Mandalee had blessed, in her pocket dimension, in case of emergency. This definitely qualified. With a prayer to Blessed Alycia, Mother of Nature, she used one to create a new ice wall to keep them trapped in the porch. Mandalee's blessing meant it was effectively frozen Holy Water, which would make it difficult and painful for the undead guards to break through, but it wouldn't stop them for long.

She knew how powerful Dreya's elite guards were. They weren't like the lumbering, unthinking ones in the grounds, still unable to work out how to break free of the ties that bound them. No magic Catriona possessed would stop them, and if they touched her…well, she didn't want to think about what would happen then. Suffice to say, when dealing with powerful undead, simply dying is often seen as a positive result.

My mother could have shifted to falcon form and flown away, but if she did that, there was no way Dreya would ever let her into her tower. Moreover, 'Get the Greatest Mage Who Ever Lived really annoyed and out for your blood' was not on Cat's to-do list for the day. If Dreya interpreted this as an actual attack, their next fight would be for real, not the fun playtime of this afternoon. Cat had to pray she could make her see reason and healing her would be a pretty good first gesture.

Catriona ran to Dreya's side and focussed all of her energy on restoring her. She told Blessed Alycia to take what she needed directly out of her own body. It would weaken her but, given the way her ice prison was breaking up, if Dreya did not recover quickly and in a favourable mood, Cat's strength would make no difference.

After an eternity, Dreya came around. The ice was beginning to splinter. The guards would be through any second.

Cat panicked. "Not an attack!" she exclaimed desperately. "Promise! Not an attack! Please call off your guards so I can get you inside!"

Dreya's head was fuzzy from the concussion, but she still managed to quip, "You're determined to get in my tower one way or another, aren't you?"

"Dreya, please!"

"You could just fly away."

Cat shook her head. "I won't leave you."

"Why not?" Dreya asked, just as the ice finally broke apart. "Be honest," she warned. "Tell the truth like your life depends on it."

"Because…" Cat began. Dreya's death knights stepped through the broken ice wall, the ghouls at their side. "Because it's my fault you got injured…"

"The truth, remember?" Dreya insisted.

"That is the truth!" she insisted. "Well," she amended, "that and I won't get what I want from you if I do."

She cringed at the admission, but Dreya just smiled.

"Now, *that* is the truth." To her guards, she commanded, "Stand down, all of you, and return to your duties! Catriona here is not to be harmed unless I specifically order it."

Her guards complied.

"I'll have to train them to recognise the difference between an attack and an accident. It's never come up before."

"You know it was an accident, then? Not an attack?"

"Of course," Dreya reassured her, choosing to remain seated on the ground for the moment. Catriona sat beside her, drained from the healing on top of all her other exertion. "You're not stupid. Reckless, yes. Stupid, no."

Cat apologised. She hadn't expected that to happen when Dreya touched her staff.

"Only happened once before," she said. "Actually, I don't even know why I got it out of my pocket dimension. It's like it *wanted* to come out. Needed, even. It's very odd."

"Well, as a further gesture of peace," Dreya said, "would you mind allowing my gardening staff to get on with their work? You've left them tied up."

Cat looked over and realised Dreya was right. "Sorry. I forgot."

She asked nature to release the undead gardeners, who simply returned to their ceaseless duties. Cat further promised to tidy up the mess she'd made with her various magics, once she had her strength back, and take the roses away from around her door.

"Leave them," Dreya told her. "In fact, why don't you move the black ones and put all three colours together? It would be a good symbol for the co-operation of the three orders of magic, which is something I'm trying to achieve with the Council. As for you, Catriona Redfletching: you beat me."

"Technically, my staff beat you," she refuted.

"Semantics," Dreya insisted. "You beat me."

"Please don't kill me!" Cat cringed.

"Kill you? That's the best contest I've had for years. I'm in your debt, and I always pay my debts. Besides, why would I kill my betrothed?"

"Your what?" Cat laughed.

"You proposed, remember? I accept."

"So, we're getting married, after all?" Cat wondered.

Dreya grinned, and replied, "Well, like you said, why don't we take it slow and start with a study date? I grant you full access to my tower's library and facilities whenever you like. How's that for a romantic gesture?"

"Really? That's amazing!" Cat cried out in joy.

Dreya tried to stand, but even with Cat's help, the world was still spinning too fast, and she promptly sat down again.

"Well then, in a romantic gesture of your own, you can carry me across the threshold."

With help from some low-level levitation from Dreya, Cat was able to get them both into her main sitting room, where they collapsed together on a sofa.

"I underestimated you," Dreya admitted. "It won't happen next time."

"Next time?"

"Well, I was hoping for a rematch…but not right now, please, dear. I've got a headache."

"I blame the door," Cat quipped. "Your door dared to attack Dreya the Dark and must be destroyed."

Dreya laughed, "I'll have it burnt, immediately." Cat gave her a meaningful look and Dreya got the message. "OK, I admit it: you are pretty funny."

"Ooh!" Cat grinned, delighted. "You think I'm pretty, too?"

"I think your magic is beautiful," Dreya replied.

Cat choked on a laugh and then blushed when she realised Dreya was serious. "Wow, thank you! No-one's ever said anything like that to me before."

"That's because other people don't see magic as I do. Magic isn't just a tool or a weapon, it's…"

"It's an art," Cat finished.

"Precisely," Dreya agreed. "Your creativity is part of what I'm trying to achieve in magic."

Dreya called one of her death knights to make some tea.

"Now, let's talk about what you need from me, Cat, and how we might advance magic, together because, thanks to you, I'm more convinced than ever that magic can do so much more."

*****

Sitting there, beside someone she dared to think of as a new friend, my mother slowly started to relax, and that, gentle reader, is the story of how Catriona Redfletching impressed Dreya the Dark.

If Catriona and Mandalee was a friendship for the ages, this was something altogether more complicated.

Chapter 18

When Catriona showed Dreya *Shifting Stars* and the other references that seemed to verify the claims made therein, Cat wasn't expecting Dreya to snap her fingers and immediately advance her research. After all, it wasn't reasonable to suppose the sorceress would have a complete inventory of the Black Tower's vast library in her head. Fortunately, that wasn't necessary.

Dreya had been interested in some of the magical research conducted by Ulvarius. That may have worried some people, but not Catriona. She didn't make the mistake others made with Dreya, in assuming she would one day become a tyrant like Ulvarius before her. That was prejudice, pure and simple: her black robes, plus her chosen residence did not automatically equal a prelude to world conquest. Dreya's interest in Ulvarius was purely academic: nobody had had access to his research before, and to Catriona, leaving that resource untapped made no sense. How could anyone know whether there was something of value unless someone was prepared to look? It seemed to Cat that although Dreya was wholly committed to Dark magic and the power it could bring her, she had not forgotten her Red robe roots. No doubt Xarnas would have told her, many times, the central tenet of the order of Balance: '*Knowledge is neutral; its application is not.*'

In this case, gentle reader, the knowledge in question came from an entry in Ulvarius' personal diary from the Day of the Lake of Tears that I have mentioned before. The day when, according to legend and his own journal (which is hardly unequivocal evidence), Lake Quernhow was formed.

A whole town wept for me this day. The baby started it, perhaps sensing how the greatness of Ulvarius was to be challenged. The rest of the town had to drown before they had a chance to spread the word and try to undermine me. Those deaths caused the ground to shake and sink beneath the waters of a brand-new lake, blessed with the souls of those I killed. It was truly magnificent.

Some higher planar creature came today to witness the glory of the power of Ulvarius. It refused to bow down to my greatness, even daring to suggest that a mage more powerful than I would one day rise. All nonsense, of course. The truth is, it secretly feared Ulvarius – I could tell – and was just using that ridiculous claim to try and make me hesitate to kill it. In the end, I let it run away so that it could warn other higher planar beings not to mess with Ulvarius in the future.

Even as the magic of Ulvarius made the whole town weep, it used some kind of staff to create a magnificent display of light in the sky in Ulvarius' honour.

Nothing will be the same, now. Now that I know my magic has caught the attention of the higher planes, everything has changed, even the sky. For today, the stars moved for Ulvarius.

Now, I daresay something struck you about that, gentle reader – besides the revelation that Ulvarius even *wrote* about himself in the third person! It certainly struck my mother.

"The stars moved for him!" she cried, breathless. "Three hundred years ago, my Angel appeared, and the stars moved for him."

"Well, I very much doubt they moved *for him*," Dreya said. "That's just his ego talking. To be honest, when I read this before, I just assumed it was a metaphor – or a delusion."

"Understandable," Cat accepted.

"But now that you've shown me your research and told me your own experiences, the similarities are too striking and repeated too often to ignore."

Comparing star charts from Ulvarius' time to more recent ones, showed a seemingly random group had once again moved out of position.

Some obvious questions naturally suggested themselves: Why did the Angel keep popping up at various times in history? Why did they conceal themselves from all but one person? And what were they doing with the Crystal Mage Staff to cause that lightshow?

"Can't answer any of those," Cat admitted, "but I do have a theory about the star shifts."

"Go on," Dreya encouraged her.

"Well, the author of *Shifting Stars* questioned whether it was the stars or Tempestria itself that was moving. He made a case for the latter, but I think he overlooked a third, more likely possibility. Maybe it's neither. Maybe the stars and our world remain unchanged in their relative positions in the heavens. Maybe it's merely our *perception* of the stars that is changing."

"You mean, something in between is filtering or refracting their light?" Dreya considered. "You're right, that does make more sense. I can't imagine any magic moving heavenly bodies around but bending light – we can do that already. It's just a question of scale. But why? What's the point?"

Cat shrugged. "And that's as far as my clever theory goes, I'm afraid. We don't even know whether the shifting stars are a goal or a side effect."

Dreya had to admit she could suggest nothing more.

"Also," Cat continued, "there's one other question that you're being really sweet not to bring up, Dreya: Whatever my Angel's been doing with this staff for goodness knows how many centuries, it must surely be important. So why in the name of Creation give it to me?"

"Maybe that's important, too?" Dreya suggested.

"Yeah, right!" Cat scoffed. "Because I'm so important!"

"You're important to me," Dreya stated, matter-of-factly, "and I happen to think I'm pretty important, so it doesn't seem an entirely unreasonable hypothesis."

Cat shook her head and offered a wry smile. "Only you could combine a compliment and self-aggrandising in one sentence."

Dreya smiled back. Cat got the impression that not many people got to see that. "Just telling it like it is."

"Well, that does lead me nicely to something I wanted to bring up," Cat said. "Since I've met you, you've talked about your interest in bringing diverse magic together to strengthen the whole, and in that context, something else has struck me about my staff."

It had occurred to Dreya, too: The readings from the Crystal Mage Staff seemed to indicate it contained diverse forms of magic, somehow bound together with higher planar energy. How, or for what purpose, the sorceress could not fathom.

Catriona snapped her out of her thoughts, speaking Dreya's name in the most solemn tone the sorceress had heard from her, and following up with a most unexpected question.

"We're friends, aren't we?" Cat asked.

Dreya looked puzzled. "I like to think so."

"But more than that – and I know it hasn't been that long – I think we have a pretty good understanding of each other."

Dreya agreed.

"So, I'm under no illusions: for you, the power will always come first."

"I won't deny that," Dreya said, "but don't for one moment imagine that means I don't…" she hesitated, unused to expressing such thoughts, "…care. I am, in point of fact, very pleased to have you in my tower and in my life."

"I know," she assured her with a smile, "and no matter how…unconventionally you say things like that, as I say, I understand you."

"What are you getting at, Cat?"

"I just want you to understand me when I say that I would never ask you to turn down a chance for power for the sake of friendship. You wouldn't, and I get that, I really do."

"Why do I feel there's a 'but' coming?"

Cat nodded. "But equally, my staff and whatever it contains, is more important to me than your friendship, if it ever came down to a choice."

"I can appreciate that," Dreya agreed, "better than anyone. I think I can see the point you're heading towards but say it anyway."

"My point is that I want to try and find a way for us to live and work together, to grow as friends, in full understanding of each other, and I want—"

"—You want assurance that I will never take power from your staff, no matter how tempted I might be."

"Exactly. I know asking you to promise is futile. Your word is not as binding as your debts. Therefore," she concluded, "I want you to think of taking power from my staff, as a debt that can never be repaid.

"Because that is the one line I would never cross," Dreya replied.

Cat shrugged. "Like I say: I understand you."

Dreya took a slow breath, in and out, in deep consideration of how to answer.

*****

Aunt Dreya was always far more multifaceted than any tyrant ever was. People don't often give her enough credit for that, but my mother always did. Cat was right that Dreya would break a promise if circumstances changed, but she did not like lies. To her mind, that was a form of debt. She would keep secrets, conceal strategic information, but first and foremost, she wanted to spearhead the building of a world of magic on Tempestria. Lies, it seemed to her, served as feeble foundations upon which to build anything.

Dreya's quest for power, Cat's search for knowledge, and their friendship for each other – all of these things were important to Dreya, and she was of one mind with Catriona in that she wanted to find a way for those things to co-exist.

*****

"Currently," Dreya said at last, "the different powers are too entangled to even think of tapping into them. I couldn't possibly control what might be unleashed. As for the future, you want to know exactly what is buried in that staff before you decide what to do with it. I completely agree. So, since I believe your word to be more binding than mine, I want you to promise me something: whenever you break through to the final layer of security and are ready to uncover what is buried, promise me I will be there, and you will include me in whatever you find. If you promise me that, I will consider myself indebted to you before the fact. Deal?"

"Deal," Cat agreed.

She and Dreya shook hands to seal it. "OK Cat, having sorted that out," Dreya said, "I have a compelling urge to shoot you."

Cat knew, when Dreya said things like that, she didn't mean it the way it sounded, but all the same, she feigned indignation as she said, "And I thought we were getting along so well!"

"Don't worry, I can turn the power of the energy beam right down. No sense in wasting power."

"Heavens forbid you should ever waste your power on me," her friend remarked.

It was Dreya's turn to shake her head in wonder. "Oh, Cat," she said, "only you could make it sound like I'm insulting you by not shooting you with a deadly energy beam."

"Well, power isn't everything, Dreya, but it's nice to know I'm worthy of yours."

"Has it occurred to you that half the things we say to each other don't make any sense, conventionally speaking?"

"Of course!" Cat concurred. "We're unconventional people. If we did make sense, that would be weird."

Deciding not to comment on that, Dreya led Cat to her training room, magically shielded to prevent any accidents due to stray magic.

Having shut the door behind her, she wasted not a moment before shooting her friend. As promised, the power was turned down so much, it was about as dangerous as any other beam of torchlight. Still, Cat treated the threat as real and responded with her Nature's Mirror, reflecting it back.

Dreya repeated the attack numerous times, sometimes with high frequency, other times with a long gap in between, so as not to give Cat any rhythm to anticipate the 'attack.' Still, every time, without fail, Cat reflected it back. Dreya switched to other magic, periodically, which allowed Catriona time to recycle the mirror back to sand.

"Interesting," Dreya remarked. "Why don't you just reuse the mirror?"

Cat picked up the most recently used one and invited Dreya to shoot her one more time. When she did so, the mirror failed to stop the torch beam and disintegrated into magical energy, leaving her with nothing to recycle back to sand.

"See?" Catriona said. "They only work once. I have to recreate all my magic from scratch every time. It's one of the drawbacks of druid magic."

"Everything has drawbacks," Dreya replied. "Conventional wizard magic takes more power than what you would need to accomplish the same thing, and as you pointed out, it requires the free use of the hands. Blood magic requires self-harm and the utmost concentration."

"What about your power words?" Cat asked, referring to the way Dreya had turned their initial contest around with nothing but the words, 'STUN,' 'BREAK,' 'SHATTER,' and 'SQUEEZE.'

Dreya explained that one of the more thought-provoking parts of Ulvarius' research had involved trying to compress writing in the language of conventional spells into what he referred to as 'power words.' He had been close, but as with blood magic, what he lacked was control.

Before explaining further, Dreya fetched a simple wooden chair from another room.

"If this broke apart, could you put it back together with your magic?" she asked. Cat agreed that would be perfectly simple. "Good," Dreya said. "I rather like it."

She set the chair down in a corner and stepped back, indicating Catriona should join her.

"If I just look at the chair and say 'Break,' nothing happens." Sure enough, nothing did. "But if I use my power word, 'BREAK'..." The chair broke apart. "Over to you, Cat," she said. Catriona used her magic, visualised how the chair looked before, and reconstructed it, flawlessly. "Now, I can't just do that again straight away, because power words aren't as simple as they look."

Dreya left the room again for a moment, returning with a pen and a sheet of paper. Then, by way of analogy, she wrote the word 'BREAK' and then folded the paper in a specific and elaborate way.

"That's like your power word," Cat understood. "Compressed, made small, but you can't just fold it any old way."

"That's one of the things Ulvarius didn't understand. In his arrogance, he thought he could make magic bend to his will as easily as he could bend people. Magic breaks if you fold it the wrong way."

"So do people." Cat remarked. "When you use your power word, then, you unfold the piece of paper, I presume."

Dreya took hold of one corner and with a deft flick of the wrist, caused the paper to unfurl once more. Catriona clapped in appreciation of the trick.

"I take it Ulvarius couldn't do that?"

"Not consistently, no. Because Ulvarius was folding the magic in random ways, the results were also random. He might intend something to break, and it wouldn't because there was no power behind the word or vice versa."

Cat's eyes widened. "You mean if you didn't fold and unfold the magic properly and you said something like, 'Let's take a break'..."

"...I could break you, yes," Dreya affirmed, "or myself. And I don't think you could use your druid magic to put you or me back together as easily as that chair. Folding the magic properly takes time and concentration. I can't risk doing it on the fly and getting it wrong. Interrupting a power word could make it backfire on me.

"I can only use a power word once, because after I use it, the magical sheet of paper I wrote it on does this..." the paper burst into flames, leaving nothing but ash. "Now, the analogy isn't perfect, because the magic will regenerate in time, but still it means every time I use a power word, I have to remake it from scratch."

"As you say, everything has drawbacks," Cat said, accepting the point.

"Yes, but the drawbacks of your druid magic are balanced by a huge advantage that I don't think you've fully realised."

Cat frowned, trying and failing to think what her friend could mean.

"I had a suspicion already, and the experiments we did today prove it."

"Prove what?" Catriona wondered, fascinated. This was so much better than her lessons in college had ever been.

"When I shoot my energy beam at you, you reflect it with your Nature's Mirror, right?"

"Yes, I've really got that down, now."

Dreya nodded. "Definitely, but there's a problem I couldn't figure out until today."

"What problem?" Cat asked, still not seeing it.

"Cat, it's impossible. You can't anticipate and block a beam of light. There isn't time to make your mirror in the fraction of a second before my beam hits you."

Cat had never thought of it like that, but she couldn't deny Dreya's logic.

"Your magic has a Temporal element. Somehow, you're manipulating Time so that the Mirror is in place exactly when you need it to be. It's the same when you mend a chair or old Renjaf's tower: you're rewinding Time. Only to a small extent, but you're doing it. Clerics can do it, too. That's how they heal injuries: they make the body revert to its pre-injured state."

"That's where it's different to druid healing," Cat agreed. "We just speed up the body's natural healing process."

"I'll take your word for that," Dreya said, "I haven't had chance to study druid magic before, but even that 'speeding up' process is temporal magic, in a way."

"But they told us at college that time magic is impossible," Cat objected.

She knew Magias, the first wizard, was supposed to have figured it out, according to legend, but since nobody could read the *Nameless Book,* she didn't know how they thought they knew that.

"That's because they're only thinking about wizards."

136

"Oh, just for a change!" Cat grumbled. "That got so annoying once I started growing my druid magic – they just wouldn't take it seriously, like wizard magic was all that matters."

Dreya agreed completely. "There isn't only one way of doing things, there never is. That short-sighted view is holding magic back. You see, Cat, your fight is my fight, especially now."

Cat found herself having to blink away moisture welling up in her eyes. "Dreya! You really do say the most unexpectedly sweet things."

Dreya shifted, uncomfortably and replied, "Yes, well, don't spread that around, OK? I have a reputation to maintain."

"Your secret's safe with me," she promised. "Although there is someone I would like you to meet."

Catriona had been living with Dreya for a month by now, and she thought it was finally time to broach the subject of Mandalee. Cat wasn't sure how the Dark sorceress would feel about having someone else spend time in her home. After all, she may not kill all intruders like the Black Tower's previous owner did, but still, she was hardly a socialite. Plus, Dark wizards and White clerics were usually an explosive combination. Even so, Cat knew it was vital that they should meet. The Crystal Mage Staff was nagging her about it with distracting persistence.

"Dreya," said Cat, taking a deep breath, "when we first met, and you grabbed my staff, you remember how it reacted?"

"I'm not likely to forget it," Dreya replied, rubbing the back of her head. "I'm sure I still have a small dent in the back of my skull!"

"Well, do you remember me saying that something similar had happened once before?"

"Vaguely, now you mention it. It's all rather hazy, I'm afraid. I was a bit dazed at the time."

"Well, I was thinking, if my staff reacted when you and I touched it, and also when my other friend and I touched it, then the obvious question is…"

"…What would happen if we all touched it together?" Dreya concluded. "Why haven't you mentioned this before?" she wondered. "Since the first time, that is."

"I wasn't sure how you'd react," Cat admitted. "My friend…she's a White cleric, and I know you're a big proponent of co-operation in magic, but still…"

"...Co-operation with wizards and druids from across the spectrum is one thing, but including clerics as well?"

"You're opposed?" Cat wondered.

"On the contrary," Dreya shook her head, "I'm fascinated by the idea. Imagine the power that could be gained from such a joining of magic! As you say, your staff seems to indicate that such a thing is possible. I'm just not sure even my ambition stretches that far. But this isn't about including clerics in the Council or some grand joining of power. This is just about me joining hands with one cleric of Light, and for the sake of this one magical experiment, your friend has my invitation if she's willing."

Cat threw her arms around her friend. "Thank you!" she cried. "You never cease to amaze me," she said, breaking the hug. Dreya seemed startled by the physical contact but did not object to it. "I really must stop underestimating you. Dreya the Dark inviting a cleric of Light into her home – whatever will the neighbours think?"

Dreya shrugged. "With any luck, it'll confuse the hell out of them."

"They might start to think you've turned nice!" Cat pointed out with a wink.

Dreya pulled a face. "There's no need to be insulting, Cat!"

*****

When Cat sent a sympathic message to Mandalee, extending Dreya's invitation, the power of the negative response almost knocked her off her feet. She'd never felt anything like this when she'd touched her friend's mind before: Mandalee was furious. At first, Catriona thought it must be Dreya or the Black Tower she was objecting to. Sympathic communication wasn't always clear on details, but when Cat projected '*friendship,*' there was no doubt whatsoever. It wasn't Dreya that Mandalee had a problem with – it was Catriona.

Honestly, Dreya's power word could not have stunned her more forcefully. So much so, a concerned Dreya gently guided her friend to the chair so she could catch her breath. When Cat tried to project '*negative understanding,*' all she got back was '*LATER*' and then she felt Mandalee slam her mental doors shut, putting Cat in mind of the time Renjaf had done that, physically, and nearly broken her nose. This hurt far more.

138

The emotional freefall, going from having such a fantastic time with Dreya to the fear that she was somehow losing Mandalee was too much for her, and she burst into tears.

Chapter 19

When Mandalee eventually turned up, she was in quite the state. Her clothes were blackened and torn, with patches of dried blood absorbed into the fabric. Her eyes were red-rimmed and bloodshot. She was limping slightly, favouring her left leg and she was visibly exhausted, practically ready to drop.

"Mandalee!" Cat cried, momentarily too frozen to move. "What happened?"

The cleric snorted, "Like you care!"

"How can you say that?" Catriona gasped. "Of course I care, I'm your friend!"

"Yeah, I used to think that," she muttered. Then when Cat moved to apply druid healing, she yelled, "Don't you dare! You don't get to erase this and say it all worked out in the end."

"What—?"

"I needed you, Catriona!" Mandalee emphasised her full name, which she'd never used since the day they met. Her message was clear: 'Your friends call you "Cat" but I'm not that anymore.' "I needed your help, but you were too busy with 'her'!" she spat, pointing at Dreya.

"Hey, don't drag me into this," Dreya objected. "It's not like I'm keeping Cat prisoner if there's somewhere else she needs to be."

"You're right," Mandalee accepted. "I almost hoped you were keeping her prisoner." To Catriona, she added, "I almost believed that was why you suddenly asked for my help."

"What? No, it's nothing like that, it's just about my staff…"

"…Of course it is!" Mandalee rolled her eyes. "It's always about your bloody staff!"

"Look, Mandalee, I only need you for an experiment—"

Mandalee laughed without humour.

"You are unbelievable! You only need me for an experiment! Otherwise, you have no use for me anymore? Well, that's perfectly clear, thank you."

"You know I didn't mean it like that!" Cat protested. Then realising the leopard was missing, she gasped in horror, fearing the worst. "Wait, where's Shyleen?"

"She'll pull through. Not that I'd bring her to this gods' forsaken place, anyway."

"Pull through? You mean she's hurt?"

"I paid for a group of druid healers to tend her."

"You paid?" Cat was incredulous. "Why wouldn't you just ask me?"

Mandalee fixed her with her bloodshot eyes, and spat, "I needed help I could rely on!"

"Mandalee, why are you acting like this?"

"Why?" Mandalee demanded, incredulously. "You know why..." she trailed off, seeing Cat's blank look. "Dear gods," she breathed, "you really don't remember, do you?"

"Remember what?" Cat asked. "Mandalee, I have no idea what you're talking about."

Mandalee finally relented to being helped inside the Black Tower, where she could sit down.

*****

Mandalee explained how she'd been contracted to kill a demon that was terrorising a town some fifty miles from the Black Tower, not far from Compton, where she'd first met Catriona. Only about an hour away as the falcon flew. From the reports, it seemed like it was a Greater Demon from one of the lower planes, and almost certainly the most powerful she had ever faced. The other odd thing was that demons of that kind didn't usually climb up from the depths on their own, which suggested it had been summoned. That, in turn, meant a wizard. With any luck, she could avoid the wizard and just take out the demon. After all, that was her job.

She had occasionally been contracted to kill a summoned mid-level demon before. Last time, the wizard himself had hired her when the demon he'd been studying broke free of his magical containment. Still, there was always the danger that a wizard could be angry at the interference, in which case, given the power of this demon, Mandalee was going to need help to defend herself. She hadn't fought a wizard before, but she knew her friend had.

She had discussed all of this with Catriona when the contract came through a couple of days ago, and although her friend had had her nose in a book, as usual, she'd said, "Sure, Mandalee. Whatever you need."

Cat frowned and searched her memory. "I think I vaguely remember saying that, but to be honest, I must not have been paying attention, because I don't recall anything about you needing my help against a wizard. Just that you were going demon hunting miles away. Mandalee, I'm sorry, but why didn't you remind me?"

"When?" Mandalee demanded. "I haven't seen you since! You've been here all the time."

"You could have contacted me sympathically," Cat suggested.

"No, Cat, she couldn't," Dreya spoke up. "The shields around my Tower block incoming mental communications. Telepathy or anything similar. Some wizards favour mental attacks over physical ones. Had you but mentioned you had this sympathic link, I could have adjusted the shield, just as I did today."

"So, what happened?" Cat asked Mandalee.

"I got lucky is what happened!"

It had taken pretty much everything Mandalee and Shyleen had to kill the demon, but the wizard was linked to it, so he knew instantly and came for her. Shyleen got between Mandalee and his first blast of magic, which nearly split the leopard in two. All the time, Mandalee was mentally screaming for Catriona who, as far as she was concerned, had promised to be there. Mandalee thought she was dead, for sure, when two figures whooshed overhead.

"It happened too fast for me to see properly, but it was most likely Daelen StormTiger fighting another of his great battles with Kullos or the dark clone – as if we don't have enough problems without them!"

"Couldn't agree more," Dreya affirmed.

Mandalee blinked in surprise, then dismissed it as unimportant.

"Yes, well, in this case, I suppose it was just as well because it distracted the wizard – only for a moment, but it was long enough for me to run him through. Then, just as I've found a druid temple to take care of Shyleen, I get a sympathic message from you, Catriona, asking me to come and help you, after you singularly failed to be there for me!"

Cat opened her mouth, but she didn't know what to say, except, "I'm so sorry, Mandalee."

"And would 'sorry' have brought Shyleen back if that wizard's magic had been just a bit stronger and killed her?"

Cat shook her head, tears welling up in her eyes. "Thank the gods it wasn't," she whispered.

"You *should* thank them," Mandalee insisted, "because that's the only reason I'm even talking to you rather than killing you."

Cat offered to fly to Shyleen immediately and make sure they were doing the healing right, but Mandalee was scathing.

"No! As I said, you don't get to undo this. Besides, I don't trust you not to get distracted by something on the way. The only reason I came here was to make sure you were OK, and this one," she pointed at Dreya, "hadn't hurt you yet."

"Hurt me?" Cat said. "What do you mean 'yet'?"

"She's Dreya the Dark. Give her time."

Dreya raised her eyebrows but did not deign to comment.

"Come on, Mandalee, that's not fa—"

"—Not fair?" Mandalee snapped. "You seriously don't want to talk to me about fair right now!" Before Cat could say anything else, Mandalee rushed headlong to ask, "I don't suppose you've found a way to do anything about this," she indicated her body, "amid all your research?"

"About what?" Dreya asked, not understanding.

As delicately as possible, Catriona explained about Mandalee's gender identity issues.

"Oh, is that all?" Dreya said.

"What do you mean, 'Is that all'?" Mandalee demanded.

Dreya held up her hands. "My apologies, I didn't intend to belittle how important this must be for you. To me, flesh is fleeting – the magic is all. I just meant, do people seriously give you grief over this?"

Mandalee nodded. "Oh yes, prejudice is still very much alive and well out there."

Dreya shook her head, her usual calm demeanour slipping to display anger. "When is the world going to actually move forward?"

With a facial shrug, the cleric replied, "I've often wondered the same thing." She paused, then, before admitting, "You know, I don't dislike you as much as I expected."

Dreya gave her a wry smile. "Well, that's progress, at least, and in return, I must say, you're the least disagreeable White cleric I've ever met."

Mandalee acknowledged that with a nod. "But you still haven't answered my question," she reminded Catriona.

Taking a deep breath and cursing herself for letting her friend down twice in one day, she had to admit that she had so far been unable to find a way to affect a permanent change. Shapeshifting wasn't the answer – not by itself. Cat couldn't hold another shape for more than a few hours. She tried to waffle about temporal magic, to turn back time for Mandalee's body to a point before puberty when it was easier for it to switch tracks and develop along the biological female line before returning it to Mandalee's current age. But she had to admit she had no idea how to do that.

"In that case," Mandalee said, "it seems to me, there's only one more thing to do before I go: this stupid experiment of yours."

"Go? Where? Why?" Cat began, then realised, "Oh, of course, to stay with Shyleen until she's better. But then you'll come back, right?" There was no immediate response. "Right?" she prompted, panic rising. She couldn't lose Mandalee. Obviously, she'd made a terrible mistake, but surely, they could work it out. Couldn't they?

Rather than answer, she just asked, "Are we doing this experiment or not?"

"Screw the experiment!" Cat insisted. "Just tell me you're coming back as soon as Shyleen's OK! Please tell me that!"

"No!" Mandalee yelled. "I've always been there for you, Catriona," she still couldn't bring herself to use her nickname. "No matter what ridiculous radical notion you got in your head, even when you said you were going to fight Dreya the Dark, I was there for you. Then the one time I asked for your help, when I needed you, you couldn't even be bothered to listen! That's not something I can get over just like that. I'm offering to help you this one last time; then I'm done."

"Not forever, though?" Catriona's tears flowed once more. "Please, Mandalee! I'm not asking you to forgive me, and I'll give you all the time you need. Please just say you'll come back when you're ready."

Mandalee shook her head. "I can't promise that. I hope so. That's all I can say." Cat opened her mouth, but the cleric cut her off. "Don't push me on this, Catriona," she warned. "There's nothing you can say right now that won't make it worse. Now, this experiment?"

Cat was floundering, her mind spinning, emotions in turmoil. She was grateful when Dreya came to her rescue, all business-like and professional. The sorceress explained how the Crystal Mage Staff had reacted to both of them individually, and the question was how it would respond to both, simultaneously. Mandalee agreed to try it, so Dreya led her two guests upstairs to her training room. Catriona said nothing. She was too terrified to even look at her friend. Former friend? It broke her heart to imagine that might be true.

In addition to the three young women, Dreya's death knight guards were also in the training room. Mandalee did not like them one bit and demanded to know what they were doing there. Dreya explained that they were a precaution, in case the staff's reaction was even more violent than before.

"If we fly apart, they are swift enough to catch us and break our fall. Frankly, it's either that or concussion."

"Concussion has never sounded more attractive," Mandalee grumbled.

"I could always tell them *not* to stop your head from going splat against my wall," Dreya offered.

Mandalee sighed, deeply and relented. "OK, let them catch me. I'm not going to risk dying. Shyleen needs me, and *I* won't let her down."

Cat flinched at the barbs that flew her way but accepted the punishment without comment. Seeing that all was ready, she took her staff out of her pocket dimension and held it in a trembling hand. Then on the count of three, Mandalee and Dreya gripped the staff at the same time.

The violent reaction they had feared did not happen. There was a kind of pull, but it seemed somehow more balanced than before. Light flared from the crystal, painting a pattern on Dreya's ceiling that looked not unlike the void storms in the Tempestrian sky. For a moment, the light began to form symbols, but they flickered and died before achieving full resolution. The staff seemed to indicate to Catriona that something was missing, but frankly, at the moment, she didn't care.

*****

The accepted historical view of this event, gentle reader, is that it was a truly momentous occasion: the first time the Original Three came together – the Three who would one day become the first Guardians of Time and Magic, and save the world many times. That's all very well for those of us who merely observe, detached, from a distance. For the three who were involved at the time, far from the beginning of something, it felt like an ending, and I'm sure the whole thing seemed utterly pointless.

Still, all relationships have their ups and downs. Even a friendship for the ages. *Especially* a friendship for the ages.

Chapter 20

Mandalee didn't stay long after that. Stepping outside into Dreya's grounds, she immediately called for her giant albatross to give her a lift back to Shyleen.

Cat couldn't let her go, though. Not without risking saying something more.

"Mandalee, wait, please," she pleaded. "Just for a minute. I want you to do one last thing for me."

"You can't be serious," Mandalee scowled.

"No, not like that. Please, hear me out."

Mandalee folded her arms.

"One minute."

"Our sympathic link. Please don't sever it. You know it's not a tracker. It won't tell me where you are or what you're doing, and I promise I won't use it to contact you. Just keep it there. Just in case. I know you have no reason to believe me, but I swear in the name of friendship if you ever need me, or want to talk, I will be there."

"For what it's worth," Dreya put in, "I have adjusted my shields so they will permanently allow full communication between you, should you wish it."

Mandalee considered for a moment and finally nodded her assent. "OK, as you say, in the name of friendship."

Catriona's relief was plain for all to see, as she grabbed hold of that lifeline of hope.

"Also, in the name of friendship," Mandalee said, "some advice. I know you won't listen to me, but I'm saying it anyway." She glared at Dreya the Dark as she said, "This one might be acting all reasonable at the moment because you've got something she's interested in, but never forget what she is. She's a Dark sorceress with a lust for power, and she would betray you in a heartbeat if it were to her advantage."

Far from being offended, Dreya agreed, "You're right, I would," she said, then with a smile at Catriona, she qualified the admission, saying, "but it would have to be the advantage of a lifetime."

Cat stared at Dreya with an open-mouthed expression, as if she'd just heard a declaration of love.

"Ugh!" Mandalee grunted, shaking her head in bewilderment. "Unbelievable!" she spat in disgust.

The gigantic bird landed, and Mandalee mounted up.

Cat leapt forward, trying to explain, but Mandalee was done and with a simple telepathic request, the giant albatross took to the sky, winging away.

Catriona wept for her lost friendship, burying herself in Dreya's soft black robes as the sorceress helped her inside and closed the door. To Cat, that felt symbolic, as if a door had just closed on a huge, important part of her life. She could only pray that one day, it might just open again.

*****

It took several days for the druid healers to restore Shyleen to full health and vitality, but soon she was ready once again to take on the demons of the world by her human friend's side. Mandalee, however, had other ideas. Although the leopard was out of immediate danger, the demon hunter's fear had morphed into a seething anger. These feelings drove her to move south to new hunting grounds, many leagues from the Black Tower and any memory of her old friend, Catriona. She also began to rethink her whole approach to demon hunting.

She'd been doing it professionally for a few years, now, and it wasn't exactly a niche profession. Thousands of demon hunters were out working every day, all across the world and stretching back an unfathomable distance into the past. All that time, effort and risk by an uncountable number of people, and what did they have to show for it? Were there fewer demons now than ever before? No. Were people now any safer from demon attack than their ancestors? No. OK, there might be no way to stop demons from coming up through the planes of reality any more than they could stop Daelen StormTiger and his kind from wreaking their brand of havoc upon Tempestria. But demons didn't just appear – not all of them, anyway. Wizards were responsible for summoning many of them.

It wasn't just Black robes, either, despite what some might say, but White robes, too. They usually claimed to be acting in the name of some imagined 'greater good,' but that was just an excuse. Red robes tended to do it only for purposes of study, but although that information had proved valuable to demon hunters, despite their best intentions, sometimes the demons got free. Then once again, people were put in unnecessary danger. If a demon killed someone, were they any less dead if it was released accidentally rather than deliberately? No.

It had to stop.

Demon hunting was futile by itself, Mandalee concluded. It was treating the symptom while ignoring the cause. Demon summoning had to stop, and since nobody else seemed to want to make that happen, Mandalee would have to do it herself.

This was the moment, gentle reader, that Mandalee the demon hunter became Mandalee the White Assassin, although the title would not come into common usage for some time. She sought out training to hone her fighting skills, as well as her unique, synergistic relationship with nature, generally, and Shyleen, specifically. Together, the pair became a force to be reckoned with.

Before long, she added a new weapon to her arsenal: a Pureblade. A sword blessed and sanctified by White clerics. It was a gift from the clerics of a temple whom she had saved from a demon attack. She loved her Pureblade. It was a thing of beauty, her most prized possession.

The first time she put it to use wasn't a contract from a human, but something Mandalee heard about from animals that were fleeing the scene. As a Cleric of Nature, Mandalee could freely converse in most of the primary animal languages and quickly learned about a 'bad man' who seemed to think it was fun to let his 'pet demon' loose on the village. It had already killed and injured many people and animals, and the wizard showed no signs of growing bored.

The demon hunter's response was to get very drunk, armed to the teeth and rush to the scene. Mandalee and Shyleen tore into the demon first because the wizard had it on a tight magical leash. If they killed the wizard first, the demon would be free and only become that much more dangerous. Mandalee's White cleric magic was physically painful to a Dark wizard, so she was able to keep him at bay until the demon was no more. Then she turned on him. He assailed her with spells, but he wasn't quick enough to track her movements. The wizard didn't seem to think it was quite so funny when he was the one about to be hurt and killed.

He begged for mercy, but Mandalee was unmoved by pity. She resolved to grant as much mercy as he had shown the innocent people of his village. For a moment, though, she did hesitate to deliver the killing blow, and the wizard lashed out, thinking to escape. The firebolt that flew from his panicked fingers was not well-directed, however, and did nothing more than singe a small patch of Shyleen's fur. But it was enough. Enough to trigger the memory of the last time, when that magical blast had almost split the leopard in two. The vision flashed through Mandalee's mind, along with her memory of screaming for help from a 'friend' who would never come.

Never again. From now on, she vowed, it would be Shyleen and Mandalee against the world, and the world didn't stand a chance as long as it tolerated people with power endangering those with none. That was the last time she would hesitate to kill in defence of those innocents. Never again.

The wizard's last few breaths were agony until that blade skewered his heart. He would summon no more demons. He would harm no-one else ever again, and if she could repeat this action enough times, then maybe one day there would be fewer demons.

Chapter 21

When Dreya came home one day, several months later, her chief death knight handed her a note from Catriona. The sorceress smiled to herself. She could guess the gist of what was written even before reading it. No doubt Cat had found an interesting nugget of information either in the Black Tower library, or even just a rumour, and she was off to investigate. She did this, from time-to-time.

Catriona wasn't big on waiting around, even to tell her where she was going or what she was planning. In fact, she wasn't big on planning at all. The plans she did have were always ridiculous and radical, and like her Nature's Mirror magic, seemed to have a way of forming on the spot precisely when she needed them. Then, as soon as she got one of these ridiculous radical ideas in her head, she would act on them. It was impulsive and reckless, but that was her nature. It was exactly that nature that had brought Catriona into her life on Midsummer's Day, and for that, Dreya was grateful beyond words.

The sorceress dismissed her guard, saying, "Looks like it's dinner for one, then."

He bowed once and left.

"What are you up to this time, Cat?" the sorceress pondered, as she headed up the stairs to read the note in her study.

No doubt it would turn into some grand adventure with which Cat would delight in regaling her, upon her return.

'*What was it last time?*' Dreya tried to recall. '*Of course,*' she realised, '*the photography incident.*'

*****

As an information trader, Catriona got wind of all kinds of things, and a couple of weeks ago, she'd somehow found out about a wizard in Gaggleswick who was experimenting with combining magic with the science of photography, to try and project a three-dimensional image from a two-dimensional photo. Cat was intrigued and decided to pay the wizard a visit. No doubt with the aid of her natural charm and wit, she'd managed to persuade him to let her help, or at least observe.

It was a good thing Cat was there, as it turned out. The subjects of the photographs on which the wizard, Asante, was experimenting, were demons. They were destined for a book intended to help demon hunters identify different kinds of denizens of hell. Asante believed that it would surely be even more helpful if the images were three dimensional and life-size. Unfortunately, his magic worked a little too well and the demonic images went on the rampage in the town. For blurry, semi-transparent constructs of light, they certainly packed a punch, and several people were killed. Demon hunters tried to kill them and failed because they weren't really alive. Nor could they be Banished down to the lower planes – they never came from there in the first place.

Thankfully, Catriona had a ridiculous radical plan, born of her endless creativity in magic. Using herself as bait – something of which Dreya would not have approved, had she known – she shapeshifted into the form of a Trickster and taunted the creatures until they all chased her. The druidess led them all down a dead end, where she immediately fused some sand into a huge curved mirror that grew to surround the monsters. The endless reflections confused them long enough for her to spring the trap. Shifting to red-banded falcon, she escaped, while Asante cast a powerful light spell that reflected off all the mirrors until the glare of the white light was too bright to look at. The intense light bleached the creatures out of existence, like a photographic film left out in the sun.

Somehow, that adventure had sparked a rumour that Catriona was romantically involved with Asante. It wasn't the first such story to circulate. For some reason, the public seemed determined that such a famous and popular figure as Catriona Redfletching must necessarily be involved with someone. They just couldn't seem to agree on who that someone was. Cat gave up denying the rumours when she realised such denial only made people even more convinced it was true.

What difference did it make what people believed? Cat knew the truth. That was all that mattered.

The incident with the runaway photographic demons was just the latest in a line of such adventures, and now, as Dreya finally sat down at her desk to read Catriona's note, it seemed she'd found another one.

Dear Dreya,
Just read something incredible in Ulvarius' journals. Perhaps the real reason why he obliterated the village at Quernhow. He was looking for something: an ancient repository of knowledge. Not a

library, as such, but more like a store, or possibly a hiding place. Most likely trying to keep knowledge safe during some long-forgotten ancient war. But that's not the best part. The best part is, according to Ulvarius – and in this case I have to say his research is pretty convincing – the books in this repository predate the void storms!

I know it's heretical to even suggest that such a time existed, but everybody thought I was crazy to believe in my Angel, so who knows?

Either way, I know you'll understand that, for me, the chance to uncover forgotten knowledge from more than a thousand years ago is utterly irresistible. No idea how I'm going to get in – Ulvarius couldn't, that's probably why he wiped out that village, to destroy any knowledge of this repository. If he couldn't have it, he was determined no-one else would, either.

But you know me – I always find a way when it's important, and as a Red robe, there's nothing more important to me than knowledge.

So yes, that's where I've gone.

See you soon.

Aye, ever yours,

Catriona

~x~

Quernhow. Dreya was sure she'd read something about that herself, recently. Rising from her seat, she crossed over to the cabinet where she kept notes from sessions of the Council of Wizards. Flicking through recent papers, she found what she was looking for.

The area surrounding the Lake of Tears, allegedly formed when the tyrant, Ulvarius, made the historic village 'cry,' had remained undisturbed since that time, three centuries ago. The story of that atrocity had always scared people away. In recent years, though, there had been a renewed interest in the area. People had begun to argue, quite logically in Dreya's opinion, that Ulvarius had committed countless acts of cruelty and barbarism across Elvaria, but that didn't stop people living their lives there today. Nor should it. So, without wishing to diminish the magnitude of the Quernhow Massacre, why should that place be any different? The Council had conceded the point and gave the go-ahead for a new village to be developed there.

However, more recently, there had been reports of undead activity from New Quernhow. It was most likely just superstition, or even an attempt to generate a kind of macabre tourism that would hardly be unique on Elvaria.

Still, Dreya thought as one of her ghoulish guards shimmered into the room to inform her that dinner was ready to be served, undead creatures did exist all over Tempestria. Ulvarius had a particular penchant for them, she knew. In fact, had he had his way, the whole world would have been populated by the undead. He had considered them infinitely more useful than the living. So, given the Ulvarius connection to Quernhow, it was plausible that he might have left a legacy beyond just the lake. Dreya knew Cat wouldn't be fazed by such reports, though, and Dreya herself was not worried as she descended the steps to the dining room.

Catriona Redfletching, the girl with a thousand ridiculous radical plans in her head, searching for a lost repository of ancient knowledge at the site of a terrible atrocity, committed by the most dangerous tyrant in modern history, perhaps infested by the undead?

What could possibly go wrong?

*****

"Thank heavens for shapeshifting," Cat said to herself as she retook her natural form on the outskirts of New Quernhow. Flying there swiftly as a falcon avoided all the hassle of a long, uncomfortable journey on horseback. She, more than anyone, understood the truth of the expression, 'free as a bird.'

Cat began wandering the streets of the village. Houses and businesses were still being constructed as the settlement was developed. The expansive Lake of Tears at the bottom of the valley, surrounded by gentle grassy slopes certainly made for a picturesque landscape. She could see the attraction, as long as one wasn't put off by the history. Cat felt it would be rather hypocritical of her to criticise, considering the history of the Black Tower that she called home. That it had once sat at the heart of Ulvarius' web of tyranny and death was all the more reason, in her opinion, to turn it into a place of beauty and life. The same was true of Quernhow.

Thinking of Ulvarius, Cat took her notebook out of her pocket dimension and went over the notes she had made regarding the wizard's exploration of this place. As always, her notes were written in her own private shorthand in case of prying eyes, so they meant nothing to anyone but her. In between the pages, she also had a few photographs of three-hundred-year-old sketches Ulvarius had made of the surrounding area, to aid her search. With these references as a guide, she believed it should be possible to tread in his footsteps. After all, three centuries may be a long time to humans or even Faery, but on a geological timescale, it was no time at all.

Ignoring the new construction, then, Cat continued to walk, all the time trying to match up the outline of the lattice of peaks and valleys to the sketches. However, Ulvarius was not known for his artistic skill, and the view from one side of the lake was similar enough to that from the opposite side, so even after an hour, she still wasn't sure which was correct.

"Ah, there you are!" came a voice, breaking her out of her inner thoughts.

Cat looked up to see a young red-robed wizard she knew at least in passing. His name was Jett and she'd first met him a couple of years back, when she'd been researching all things related to *Shifting Stars*. As usual, her research had told her that he had a rare text that could be useful to her, so she'd gone to visit him. Thankfully, there had been no need to demolish his home, as he was only too pleased to exchange knowledge. He was an archaeologist by profession, and as such he, too, was often searching for rare texts to advance his research. Therefore, he told Cat he would be happy to dig out the book she wanted to borrow, if only she would try and find what he was looking for, in return. She didn't just try – she succeeded.

As soon as she'd come across Ulvarius' notes about this store of ancient knowledge, she immediately thought of Jett. After all, what was the point of knowledge without people to share it with? So, she'd sent him an urgent magical message, inviting him to join her on what she had described, without hyperbole, as 'the archaeological find of a lifetime.'

Grinning, he opened his arms wide and said, "Hey, Cat!"

"Jett!" she cried, matching his smile and embracing him. "How'd you get here so fast?"

"Asked a friend to teleport me."

Teleportation may be faster than flying, Catriona conceded, but it meant missing out on all the scenery along the way, and the sheer joy of flight itself.

Realising they were attracting attention, Cat said, "Better break the hug, or people will start saying you're my new wizard lover!"

Stepping back, Jett nodded. "Yeah, I heard about you and Asante."

"Oh? Do you keep tabs on all my love interests?"

"That would be a full-time job, wouldn't it?" Jett laughed. "But most of your love interests don't come with photos."

Cat blushed slightly and agreed, "Yes, you're right, photos of me with my 'lovers' are much rarer, but that one was not at all what it looked like. The camera just went off accidentally and the angle was…unfortunate." She shook her head to clear her mind of distractions. "Why am I even explaining? I didn't ask you here to talk about rumours," she said. "Well," she amended, "not rumours about me, but rumours about an ancient repository of knowledge buried around here, somewhere."

When she explained in detail, Jett was clearly as excited as she was. "If we could really find it," he said with a crooked smile, "that would be well worth putting up with a few rumours about being your new lover!"

Doing her best to act offended, Cat replied, "I don't even know how to take that, so I shall rise above it."

Of course, Jett couldn't read her notes, and she wouldn't translate them word-for-word – that would defeat the object of her secret language – but she gave him the gist of what they said. In concert with her photos of Ulvarius' drawings, they agreed on a place to start, although they still weren't sure which side of the lake they were supposed to be on. Decision made, Jett felt they ought to share at least some of their plan with whoever was in charge of the local community.

That person turned out to be a lady called Solana, who the locals acknowledged as Community Leader. It was an unofficial post. Unlike somewhere like Gaggleswick, New Quernhow wasn't yet large enough to have a local government. She was simply the first resident here, having been involved in the original petition to form this settlement. As such, she knew all the right contacts if there were any issues the residents wished to address.

Cat and Jett explained, in broad terms, that they were in possession of certain documents that suggested there might be something buried underneath New Quernhow that predated even Ulvarius' reign of terror. The area they were intending to begin excavation was well away from any buildings in the fledgeling town, but as a courtesy, they felt they ought to ask permission before starting work.

"What exactly do you hope to find?" Solana asked.

Jett opened his mouth, but seeing Cat shake her head, slightly, he let her jump in with, "I'm sorry, but we'd prefer to keep that to ourselves for now, if you don't mind."

If she was right and there was such a repository here, the place would have to be protected and secured. The last thing she wanted was for a crowd to burst into the place and potentially destroy what they found. Besides, knowledge could be dangerous.

Accepting her wish to keep the details confidential, Solana agreed, "Well, whatever it is, I wish you luck. It would certainly be nice if this place could be known for something other than a three-hundred-year-old massacre. And the least said about the so-called hauntings, the better."

"Hauntings?" Jett wondered.

Solara explained about the rumours that had begun to circulate, but Cat wasn't worried.

"There are plenty of undead around where I live," she said. "They don't bother me anymore."

"Besides," Jett put in, "the rumours are probably just that: rumours, and we all know how ridiculous they can be, eh, Cat?" he added with a wink.

Cat gave him a playful shove for his trouble.

*****

Returning to their chosen site, Cat began to use her earthshaper magic to gently tease the ground apart. At the same time, Jett gathered some local stones and placed them in a large ring around the area, which Cat grew into walls to keep people and animals out. Returning her focus to the ground, she took her time, peeling back a layer at a time, not wanting to destroy any vital clues that Jett's expert eye might spot.

After a few hours, the daylight began to fade, and they decided to leave their work for the night. The village didn't have any lodging houses, but Solara managed to find a couple of local families who were willing to take them in.

The painstaking process of digging continued for five days until at last, Jett shouted, "Stop! I think I see something!"

Crouching down, he moved some more soil aside with his bare hands so he could feel what he thought his eyes had seen: stone. It wasn't just compressed earth, but a stone slab, and given the way it curved, there was no question – it was the roof of an artificially constructed tunnel heading directly towards the lake.

"Of course!" Cat cried. "That's why he did it! That's why Ulvarius killed all those people in that particular way and formed the Lake of Tears in that spot."

Jett caught on saying. "You think, the repository is—"

"—right under the lake!"

In his journal, which Cat conceded was hardly unequivocal evidence, Ulvarius had been quite clear that he had found the lost repository he was looking for. Of course, he could have been lying, but if so, since it was his own private journal, he would only have been lying to himself. Again, the idea that the tyrant might have been self-delusional was far from unreasonable, but if he was going to lie to himself about finding it, why admit that he had been unable to get inside?

"You're right," Jett said, "it makes sense. An artificial lake with no runoff would naturally accumulate all kinds of silt and soil and debris to cover anything that might lay beneath."

Cat nodded. She also knew that, according to reports from periods of drought when the water level was lower, the lake was filled with the skeletal remains of Ulvarius' victims.

"Not exactly the kind of place that makes you think, 'Let's go skinny dipping,' is it?" Cat remarked.

Chapter 22

"Now," Jett said, "a responsible archaeologist would excavate this entire site to try and find the original entrance."

"We could do that," Catriona agreed, nodding. "Then again, I do have stoneshaper magic."

"So, you could carefully part the stone and we could levitate down into the tunnel through the roof."

Cat made a rude noise. "Levitate? So undignified. I'll use my Windy Steps, thank you. But your point still stands."

"Well, what are you waiting for," her wizard friend asked with a cheeky grin, "a responsible archaeologist?"

"Don't know any, I'm afraid," Cat grinned back.

"Me, neither."

Catriona did as he had suggested and a moment later, they were inside the ancient tunnel.

"Make yourself useful," she said, "and make us some light."

He did as she asked, illuminating their surroundings just enough for them to see where they were putting their feet, while keeping the area beyond in shadow. If they found what they were looking for, the contents could be sensitive to light, and he didn't want to risk causing damage. On the other hand, if they couldn't see properly, they could do even more damage by blundering into things or stepping on something delicate.

In keeping with Catriona's theory, they followed the tunnel, slowly and carefully in the direction of the lake. They had to walk in single file, but at about ten feet high, it was perfectly comfortable. There was no need to mark their passage, as it simply continued in an unbroken straight line, sloping ever downwards.

They walked in silence, all joking suspended, as if it might disturb the blessed sanctuary of which this place somehow spoke. In time, the passage ended in a wooden door.

"If this place is as old as it appears to be, how come this door looks brand new?" Jett wondered, gently probing it with his magic. "Some kind of preservation spell?"

"No," Cat replied, shaking her head. "Or maybe yes," she reconsidered, "but not the way you mean. The wood looks fresh because it's still living."

"What? How?"

"No idea," Cat replied, "but I can feel it through my druid magic. The wood of this door is every bit as alive as that of any tree. It may not be growing in the sense of getting larger – it's the same size it's always been – but it is constantly rejuvenating itself.

"Astonishing!" Jett breathed.

His light caught an inscription above the door. That was not so well preserved, and some of the letters had faded over the course of centuries. All they could make out for sure, was:

IN LOV　G　ME　　RY　　F　ALYCIA

But it was still legible enough to deduce the intent.

"Surely, 'In Loving Memory of Alycia,' yes?" Cat whispered, reverently. "That's not just the half-Faery druid in me talking, is it? That's what it says, right?"

"That's what it looks like to me," Jett agreed.

Blessed Alycia, Mother of Nature, was a revered figure to Faery, wielders of nature magic and just nature lovers in general.

There was another line underneath, in a smaller script that had suffered even more erosion over time, such that only a single portion was still legible and then just barely.

E　L　ST　W

The rest was lost to the passage of time and guessing the meaning was futile. There simply wasn't enough to go on.

Logically, the next step was to open the door, but that proved to be easier said than done. Jett and Cat lent all their weight to the task, but the door would not budge an inch. Catriona tried her woodshaper magic, but the door remained untouched. She switched to stoneshaper magic to try and create a gap *around* the door, but it seemed whoever built this had thought of that, so it failed.

Jett had been reluctant to try anything with his wizard magic, not wanting to risk causing damage, but they seemed to have run out of alternatives.

"I won't blast it," he said, "but I will try a focussed fire spell. That should burn through the wood, but I'm not much of a multi-tasker, so would you mind taking over with the light?"

"Alright," Cat agreed, and took her Crystal Mage Staff out of her pocket dimension, causing it to cast a blue light over the door.

Jett cancelled his own light spell and cast out a thin jet of intense flames. He sustained it in one spot for two or three minutes, but the wood didn't even begin to char.

"Fireproof wood?" he breathed in wonder, as he cancelled the spell.

"I don't think it even warmed up!" Catriona marvelled, stepping forward to carefully place her free hand on the door. "I guess this is why Ulvarius couldn't get in." The instant her hand touched the wood, however, some kind of mechanism on the other side clicked and the door swung open. "What the—" she cried, jumping back.

"Maybe it likes you?" Jett suggested.

"Maybe," Cat allowed, "or maybe it's this," she said, holding up her staff.

"Your staff?"

Cat nodded, "Or perhaps the combination of magic and higher planar energy within it."

"Why would that work?" Jett wondered.

"It's just a guess," she shrugged.

She supposed all that mattered was that they had gained entry. The how and why weren't really important.

Stepping through the now open doorway, Cat found her breath taken away by the sight of a cavernous space carved into the bedrock of Quernhow. Carved with magic, druid magic like hers. She recognised the signs. Inside, were rows upon rows of shelves filled with books, scrolls and other documents. It wasn't just one room, either, but many adjoining ones. Despite this, however, those ancient people had run out of space and had been forced to stack yet more volumes on the floor. Many of those stacks towered above their heads. She could see why Ulvarius had referred to it as a 'repository of knowledge' – calling it a library wouldn't do it justice.

Into the silence, Jett whispered, "Well, Cat, you promised me the archaeological find of a lifetime."

Cat raised a quizzical eyebrow. "Disappointed?"

He answered her clearly facetious question with an entirely serious, "Yes."

Cat frowned, incredulously.

"I'm disappointed that I have only a single human lifetime," he clarified, with tears in his eyes, "because I doubt that's enough time to even catalogue what's down here, let alone study the contents!"

Cat moved over to him and embraced him. "I know what you mean," she said. "At best, I hoped to find a small hidey-hole, maybe a few dozen books if I was lucky. I never imagined all this!"

Jett gently broke the hug, stepping away to try and come to terms with what he was seeing.

Catriona, too, began to wander around, stepping carefully around the stacks, not knowing where to begin. After a few moments, though, something caught her attention: a book of star charts. It was sitting apart from everything else, propped up on the floor with its content on display, as if somebody long ago wanted this to be the first thing any future visitor would see.

"Well, whoever you were, it worked," the druidess said softly, as if the spirit of that long dead individual might hear her, if only she were quiet enough.

Not wanting to even risk handling it, she called Jett over and asked him to use some of his levitation magic on the book.

"Good idea," he approved. "The less we touch things, the better."

The star charts contained within those pages were astonishingly detailed, putting current efforts to shame. Even more extraordinary was that the charts all seemed to be in pairs, like before and after images.

Before and after what, was abundantly clear, for the left-hand page was completely free of void storms. They didn't exist before, only after what the title referred to as:

THE GREAT STAR SHIFT

The two companions began to risk touching a few other volumes at random. It turned out there was nothing at all fragile about them. This time, it was preservation magic, just as Jett had suggested earlier. Enough to protect the books from just about anything short of wilful damage, fire or flood.

They adopted the policy of flicking through a few pages to try and gain an essence of what the book was about, before returning each one to the place they found it, just in case there was some kind of system in place that currently eluded them.

Ulvarius, evil tyrant though he was, had been right about this repository of knowledge. These books were definitely from a time more than a thousand years ago, before Year Zero, and it was obvious that they were describing a world that was very different to the one they knew.

"Lost world!" Cat blurted out, suddenly.

"Random," Jett remarked.

"No, it's not," she refuted. "It's the inscription on the door – The Lost World."

"The world that was lost when the void storms began," Jett realised. "The time of this Great Star Shift. I think you're right.

"And I'll tell you something else," he continued. "That book of star charts is obviously from shortly after it happened, which, relatively speaking, probably makes it the most modern thing in this whole place!"

Catriona's jaw dropped. She hadn't thought of it like that. Calin's Tower, overseas, was the foremost public library of knowledge in the whole world. It was about a hundred and fifty years old. Some of the books in the Black Tower's library dated back four centuries. But this book of thousand-year-old star charts, was probably the most modern thing here. Overcome by the enormity of it, she had to sit down for a moment to catch her breath, cradling the precious book of star charts in her hands.

Some of the books they opened had hastily written notes on the inside cover. The meaning wasn't always clear, but the tone was one of urgency.

While Catriona puzzled over that, Jett explored further until he came across another door, identical to the one through which they had entered.

According to Ulvarius' map there was only one entrance, but then, he supposed, having found one, since he couldn't get in, what would have been the point of searching any further?

"I wonder if it needs your staff to unlock it from the inside?" he said.

Cat heard him open it, which she supposed answered his question, but as he did so, he immediately screamed for help.

Thrusting the book into her pocket dimension, she rushed to his side, where she saw him frantically pushing against the door with all his strength, trying in vain to shut it while through the gap were half a dozen skeletal limbs, pushing back. She added her own weight to the door, desperate to get it to shut, while using woodshaper and stoneshaper in concert to try and seal the doorway shut. It wasn't working, but it did buy time.

"The passage!" Jett gasped. "It's full of undead creatures!" and by the looks of what was trying to squeeze through, it wasn't just undead people, but animals, too.

All at once, Cat put it together. More than three hundred years ago, Ulvarius had come here, found the repository and tried to gain entry. He probably tried for a long time but ultimately, he was forced to give up. He laid waste to the entire town, not only in revenge, but also to prevent knowledge of either the repository itself or his failure, from spreading. But, having a penchant for creating undead creatures, he hadn't wasted the living resources. He had kept them here on guard, just in case anybody else ever found the place. Until now, Cat and Jett had got lucky – because the maps weren't entirely clear, they had found a second entrance that Ulvarius didn't know about. But as soon as Jett opened the door they had been left to guard, all the undead had reanimated almost immediately, and set about following their three-hundred-year-old instructions to kill anyone they saw.

But there was no way that passage was large enough to accommodate the entire human and animal population of a town. So where were all the rest?

"The lake!" Cat cried out in realisation.

"Dear gods!" Jett caught on. "The Lake of Tears is full of the remains of people and animals from Ulvarius' time. An undead army lying dormant…until now!"

"And we've woken them up! They'll kill everyone up there! It'll be a massacre, just like before!"

"What can we do?" Jett asked, desperately.

"How do people usually destroy the True Undead *en masse*?" Cat returned. "Holy Water!"

Clerics used it all the time. It wouldn't destroy them by itself, but normally, it would weaken them to the point where conventional magic or steel could finish them off. But these weren't just any undead, they were created by Ulvarius for the single-minded purpose of guarding this place for eternity. He would have made them to last. When Dreya took the Black Tower, she managed to wrest control of the undead guards from Ulvarius' magic, but she didn't destroy them.

164

In the years since, she had experimented on a few of them to find the best method of destroying them, should it ever be necessary and she had confirmed that Holy Water was the best way, although it took a long time.

"Exactly!" Jett shot back. "Know any clerics you can call on, quickly?"

"Not anymore," Cat answered, sadly, thinking of Mandalee. Still, that thought triggered a memory. "But if I'm lucky," she said. "If I'm really, really lucky…"

She opened her pocket dimension, closed her eyes and made a wish. If she was right, salvation would come to hand. If she was wrong, well, she supposed she could call Dreya. She might be able to get here in time to rescue her – she might even save Jett – but that wouldn't help everyone else.

"Please let me be right!" she prayed.

She felt something fly into her hand, a small glass vial, and quickly closed her fingers around it. It was cold to the touch, she thought as she closed her pocket dimension, but she'd never felt anything more beautiful.

Catriona opened her eyes, daring to look.

"Yes!" she cried. She was right: she still had a single vial of water Blessed by Mandalee. Tears in her eyes, she brought it to her lips and kissed it. "Oh, Mandalee. Even now, you're here for me. In spite of everything."

"How's that little thing going to help?" Jett demanded, trying to force the undead limbs back with his magic.

He was right. Time for sentiment later. Now the people of New Quernhow needed her to act.

"I have a ridiculous radical plan," she told him, "and you're going to hate me for it."

"Why?"

"Because I already hate myself for thinking it!"

Even as she spoke, the door finally gave way, and undead by the dozen, the score, came pouring into the chamber. Jett fought them off with his magic as best he could, as they retreated through the alcove into the previous chamber, which Cat tried to block with an ice wall.

Knowing that wouldn't hold them back for long, Cat's mind was racing, trying to fill in the details. She needed to do something that had never been done before. Something clerics would say was blasphemy:

replicate Holy Water. She could replicate regular water in her sleep, but Holy Water had to be Blessed by clerics. Or so they said. Cat didn't believe it. There had to be a way.

"How does Holy Water work?" she pondered, mostly to herself. "Strip away the religion, and how does it physically work?"

Well, she considered, druid healing sometimes used water. For some infections, or for healing multiple patients at once. The magic was suspended in the water, so as the water penetrated the skin, so did the magic. Then that magic could draw the infection out of the body. Holy Water must do the same.

"The undead absorb the water, then the magic can get to work on them from the inside! You can call it a Blessing; you can call it anything you like. But it's just magic at a particular frequency, to which the animation magic is susceptible."

It was the same phenomenon that meant Mandalee's magic caused Dreya pain. It wasn't a matter of good magic versus evil magic. Magic wasn't good or evil. Magic, like all power, like all knowledge, was neutral. It was the application that made it good or evil.

Dreya wasn't evil, either, just because she was aligned with the Dark. The idea that Light was good, and Dark was evil was lazy thinking. There were many good deeds done in the shadows, and much evil done in the light of day.

The reason White-aligned cleric magic was painful to a Dark-aligned wizard was nothing more than a clash of incompatible frequencies. Like music that was full of discordant notes. Disharmonious.

"So? How does that help?" Jett demanded.

"It helps because now I know I can definitely do it and I hate myself even more!"

Her ice wall shattered under the relentless assault.

"Give them one last push with magic and then run out the door we came in!" Cat ordered. "On three…One…Two…Three!"

With their different magics, they created a powerful gust of wind that pushed the undead back about twenty feet. It also knocked over whole piles of books and papers that had stood undisturbed for a millennium. The companions ran for the door as fast as they could.

As Cat ushered Jett out, he cried out in warning, "Look out!"

Cat yelped as she felt something grab her ankle: it was a disembodied skeletal hand. She tried to strike it with her staff, but it wasn't enough to make it let go. "Get ready to close the door!" she yelled. She had an idea, but they needed to be fast.

The druidess quickly shifted to falcon form, leaving the hand nothing to hold onto, and flew out before it could try again. Jett slammed the door shut as she shifted back, staff in hand. Pressing her palm against the wooden door, she closed her eyes and spoke softly to the spirits of that place.

"You recognised me, or my staff, or something, before. Please recognise it again and seal this door." To her relief, the mechanism clicked into place. "Thank you, and I'm sorry," she whispered.

Jett was distraught at the thought of the undead on the rampage in there, tearing all that ancient knowledge to shreds. "You're right, I hate this plan," he told Cat.

The druidess shook her head. "Haven't even started yet!"

"But you've got a way to get them out, right?" She didn't reply. "Right?" he tried again, desperately.

She couldn't even look him in the eye as she said, "I'm sorry."

Chapter 23

Without another word, Catriona shifted to falcon form and flew away. Jett could levitate himself out the way they came, but she didn't have time to wait for him. As she flew up and over the lake, she could see how the water was already churning as the undead stirred and began to rise from their aquatic bed. The people of the village, seeing what was happening, began screaming and running away from the lake. Now that they been awakened, the undead would kill every last person, just as Ulvarius ordered three centuries ago. Others would come; other settlers, friends and relatives, and the undead would kill them, too.

More than likely, some people would escape, but the undead could be very literal when it came to following orders. If they had been told to kill anyone with knowledge of this place, they would hunt down those who escaped. When the undead reached the next town, they would have no way of knowing who the escapees might have told, so they would slaughter the whole town, just in case, and use their innate magic to turn many of those people into True Undead, like them. Thus, their numbers would swell as they spread like a plague to overrun more and more settlements.

And Catriona knew all those deaths would be her fault because she woke them up. Jett may have opened the door, but he never would have been there if not for her. She couldn't let this happen. She had to stop it here and now.

Staying in her falcon form, then, she caused the water around the edge of the lake to rise up into a cylinder of ice that would hopefully keep the village safe for a few moments, while she did what she had to do. Underground, the undead would try to escape the passage they were in, and no doubt, given time and their numbers, they would tunnel their way out. She wasn't going to give them that time.

Coming to a halt, high above the Lake of Tears, she shifted back, standing on one of her Windy Steps. The undead were hacking at her ice wall and cracks were beginning to form. Given the size of the lake, there could be hundreds of undead down there, maybe thousands, and no wall of ice or even rock could stand against that for long, so she needed to hurry.

She focussed her magical senses on the vial of Holy Water in her hand, probing, analysing.

"Now, Blessed Alycia," she said aloud, "I really need your help to save all these people. I need you to take my analysis of the water in this vial, and when I pour it into the lake down there, I need you to make all that water like this. This has to work. It *will* work."

Taking a deep breath, she kissed the vial once more and then broke it, tipping out the contents. As the Holy Water fell like raindrops, Jett levitated over to join her.

"What are you doing?" he asked.

"Watch," she said, determined that her magic would function as she envisioned it.

There was nothing visible about the change to the water, but all of a sudden, the undead began writhing in silent agony as the replicated Holy Water seeped into their bones, attacking the magic that animated them. As long as they were immersed, they would be weakened, but if they should escape, it wouldn't take them long to dry out. It was imperative they should be contained until the `Blessing` magic could overcome the animation spell. Unfortunately, there was no way of telling how long that would take. Many years. Decades. Maybe centuries.

"That's all very well for that lot," Jett conceded, "but what about the ones underground? They're still strong enough to break out and when they do, even if these are still contained, they'll shatter your ice walls, and all this will be for nothing."

"I know. This is the part where you hate me."

"Why? What are you going to do? I still don't get it!"

"Jett," she said, "I think you're forgetting where we are. What's below us?" she prompted.

"The Lake of Tears," he answered.

"And what's below that?" she asked. "What's *directly* below that?"

At last, the wizard caught on. "No!" he gasped.

Cat nodded, sadly. "I told you, you'd hate me."

"You can't!"

"I have to."

The lake was directly above the ancient repository, like an enormous bath full of Holy Water. All she needed to do was let the plug out. Put a big enough hole in the bottom and all the undead would be flushed down to join their fellows. The repository was easily big enough. The water would flood every chamber and the adjoining tunnels, drowning the undead. When the lake was no more, she could fill in the hole, reseal the tunnels and the undead would be trapped.

"But all that water…all those books! They'll be destroyed. Ruined! All that knowledge, lost."

"I know," Cat nodded.

As she'd said, she hated herself for thinking it, but there was no other way. Even if some scraps miraculously survived, there was no way to be sure how long it would take for every last undead creature to become inert, permanently at rest. If somebody tried to open it up, believing it had been long enough, and they were wrong, they would be killed and the undead would escape their watery prison. No. The repository would have to remain sealed and flooded, effectively forever.

"This would always have happened," Cat said. Was she trying to convince Jett or herself? "Sooner or later, somebody would have uncovered that repository and the undead would have risen to stop them. Ulvarius made sure of that. Three hundred years ago, a petty, jealous man learned of that place, full of ancient knowledge, and he decided that if he couldn't have it, nobody could. Not ever."

"But he doesn't have to win!" Jett insisted. "We could let the undead out, put together an army, fight them out here. Then the repository would be safe."

"At the cost of how many lives?" Cat challenged him.

"But you're not with the Light!" Jett protested. "You're not a hero. You're a Red robe, like me. You're supposed to value knowledge above all else."

"I know," Cat insisted, making it clear she wasn't going to change her mind.

"Those books must have been buried for a reason," Jett pointed out. "Those ancient people wouldn't have gone to all that effort unless it was important. You saw the notes inside some of those books. They were trying to tell us something. For all we know, the knowledge they contain could be vital to the future, vital to the world!"

"You think I don't know that?" Cat shot back, venomously. She'd replayed Jett's argument in her head a dozen times before he spoke the words. It was a perfectly valid point. He could easily be right. By saving the present, she could be condemning the future. How could she know?

"You think I want to be making this choice?" Her voice cracked on the words. She wasn't qualified to make this choice, she sure as hell

170

wasn't authorised, but the fact remained she was the one here making it. "If it were just a matter of our lives, I'd agree with you," she told him. "I know if it were just me, I would give my life to protect that knowledge, to preserve it for future generations as our ancestors did a thousand years ago. I could make that choice and so could you, but what about everyone else? I can't make that choice for them. I don't have the right!"

She couldn't know the future. All she could do was deal with the situation in front of her and do the right thing as best she could.

"I could stop you," Jett told her in a quiet voice, filled with menace. A fireball flared and grew in his hand.

"Then do it now," Cat replied, "because I'm out of time."

Even in their weakened state, some of the undead in the lake were on the verge of breaking through her ice wall. It was time to pull the plug.

She worked her earthshaper magic, ripping the lakebed apart, delving deeper until she reached the roof of the tunnel. As she switched to stoneshaper, Jett's expression darkened further. He drew his hand back, ready to unleash his magic at Catriona.

"Don't make me do this!" he growled.

"Do as you will," was Cat's only reply.

She didn't move. Didn't try to stop him. She needed every bit of focus she could muster to execute her plan. If he chose to execute her in the process, well, maybe it was no more than she deserved.

At the crucial moment, however, Jett faltered and extinguished the flames.

"I can't," he said, shaking his head. "As much as I hate you for this, Catriona, I can't murder you and you're right, I can't let others die, either."

The druidess broke through at last and the lake began to drain away. She widened the gap as much as she dared, and then switched her focus to her wall, replenishing it and contracting its dimensions to force the undead around the edge to plunge down the plughole, down into the depths.

Catriona was in tears as she worked, weeping for all that lost knowledge and the efforts of countless people, so long ago, who tried to preserve it. Effort that was now wasted, all because of the vindictive actions of one small-minded man that forced her, a simple half-Faery druid girl to do this to save lives.

A while later, when it was safe once more, community leader Solana approached Catriona as she stood exhausted on the bank, panting and leaning heavily on her staff.

Actually, she considered, could it still be 'the bank' if there was no longer a lake?

"You saved our village!" Solana cried, gathering Catriona up in an embrace.

"That's one way of looking at it," Jett grumbled.

"But what did you do to the lake?" she asked, stepping away.

"I drained it," Cat answered, frowning in puzzlement at the question.

"Obviously," Solana rolled her eyes, "but I mean, before that!"

"Oh, replicated Holy Water," Cat replied.

Solana raised her eyebrows. "I didn't know that was possible."

"Neither did I until today," Cat admitted. Then, catching Jett's meaningful look, she excused herself, saying, "Look, we'd better go. There's nothing more we can do here."

She turned to leave, but Solana caught her arm to ask one last question. "What did you find down there?"

Cat opened her mouth, but Jett got in first, smoothly, to assure her, "Oh, just some ancient tunnels. Interesting, archaeologically speaking, but nothing worth facing Ulvarius' legion of the undead for."

Solana accepted that with a smile and a nod, and then shook both their hands before heading off to see what she could do to restore peace and order to her village.

When she was well out of earshot, Jett explained, "We can't tell anyone what we really found. The temptation could be too great for some."

Cat nodded. She understood that all too well. The lure of this place had been so strong for her. It was in her nature; she just had to know. She couldn't help wondering how much trouble that attitude might get her into in the future. She didn't dare tell him about the one thing that she had saved. The book of star charts that was now inside her pocket dimension.

"Much as I don't like it," Jett continued, "Solana's right: you did save this village, perhaps the whole of Elvaria, and knowing you, you'll probably go on to save the world."

"Don't be ridiculous," she insisted, blushing. "I'm just a simple half-Faery druid girl." Frankly, she didn't want that responsibility.

"If you say so," Jett shrugged. She might not believe it, but he did.

Then, to Catriona's surprise, the wizard briefly hugged her.

"I don't hate you," he assured her as he pulled away again. "At least, I won't once the open wound has had time to scab over. But it would probably be best if we didn't see each other again. Sorry, but your face would always remind me of what was lost today, reopen this wound and I don't think I could bear that. Besides, otherwise, people might start to wonder if we really did find something here."

"That's OK," Cat accepted. "You know what the rumours are like. You'll just end up being the latest in a long line of wizard lovers I've apparently had and broken up with."

Giving her a crooked smile that failed to reach his eyes, he suggested, "There is a way we could help those rumours along, if you're willing."

When he explained, Cat replied, "That's almost as bad as one of my ridiculous radical ideas. Let's do it, but just before that, if I'm not going to see you again, can I just say, thank you and, well, I suppose, have a good life."

"You, too," he replied. "No hard feelings. Ready?" he asked.

Cat nodded.

Jett kissed her, full and long, and then, when she was sure they had attracted plenty of attention, Cat pulled away and slapped him.

With a huff, she shifted to falcon form and flew away, leaving Jett to find a horse and travel home the conventional way.

*****

That evening, when Dreya returned to the Black Tower after a Council session, she could immediately see Catriona's haunted look as she gazed with unseeing eyes at what appeared to be a book of star charts.

"What's wrong, Cat?" she asked. "You look like you've seen a ghost."

"Bit more than ghosts, I'm afraid, Dreya," she replied with a weak smile. "Legacy of Ulvarius."

Despite what Jett had said, she had to tell Dreya. That repository would hold no lure for her. There was no power in it.

*****

"Did I do the right thing?" Cat asked when she reached the end. "I mean, Jett had a point: I'm aligned with the Balance. That's supposed to mean knowledge first."

"Light, Dark, Balance – Life, Power, Knowledge," Dreya began. "Are they so different in the end? To me, it's just a question of emphasis. What's the point of knowledge or power without people to use it? What's the point of living without knowledge of reality, and the power to change it? That's what I'm striving for with the Council – better co-operation between the factions so that we can move this world forward together. As I once told Laethyn, when I say I want to be the Greatest Mage Who Ever Lived, I want that to mean something. Tyrants like Ulvarius and threats like the shadow warriors cannot be allowed. The loss of that ancient repository is a sad victory for Ulvarius but letting his undead army loose would have been worse. You absolutely did the right thing, and you did it, as always, in a way only you could have possibly dreamed up. I'm proud of you."

*****

In the days that immediately followed, gentle reader, my mother viewed that ancient book of star charts as a prized possession. Unfortunately, in practical terms, without any real context, it proved to be of little use, so after about a week, it simply sat untouched on a shelf. It would be many years before its value was truly realised.

There were many more grand adventures for my mother over the next year or two, though none quite as harrowing as the story I just told. Through it all, however, she could find no trace of her old friend, Mandalee. True to her word, she wasn't actively trying to find her, but she never strayed far from her thoughts. Through her sympatic link, she could take solace in the knowledge that her old friend was alive somewhere. She just thought it would be nice to at least hear something about what her life was like, now.

My mother was going to have to wait a while longer, yet, but one day, when the world was held in the balance, their paths would cross again.

*****

It's a great pity that my mother was forced to flood that repository, a thousand years ago. The knowledge we could have gained over the centuries might have told us much that would be relevant even in my time. If those books were recorded when the void storms started, they might also have documented how and why. Then we might have learned how to stop them.

I can see them now, as I gaze out of my window once more, burning brightly in the sky, though currently frozen in Time. In the millennium since my mother's time, though they continue to wax and wane, their average intensity has gradually increased to the point where they can cause tremors and quakes, reactivate otherwise dormant volcanoes and cause flash floods. The magical techniques we now possess are usually enough to mitigate the worst of the damage and save lives, but for how much longer? How long before they grow too powerful for anyone do anything about it? How long before the tidal forces they generate rip our world apart? According to official calculations, we have, at best, about ten years. But others can't see Time like I do. They can't see the way the void storms are tearing the fabric of our world apart. I can't prove it, but I know we don't have ten years. It's less than that. A lot less.

Unfortunately, we are unable to expend the resources we would need to combat this danger, because there is an even more imminent threat.

I wasn't there when it began, that summer evening, but I've seen it many times, since. Too many.

The gleaming city of Walminster, home to more than a million residents and thousands of visitors, is much changed from my mother's time. Only the historic Council building, with its Protected status, remains the same.

Gone are the standard medieval cottages, smoky chimneys and horses for transport. Residential buildings can be whatever shape, colour and style the owners wish. A few change that night, perhaps to

175

make room for a new arrival. In the sky, transport pods race along roads that appear only when they need to, and teleport pods provide more long-distance options for those who can't teleport themselves. A holographic concert is underway in the nearby arena, beamed live from another world. Others seek their own entertainment with smaller displays that appear above the palm of their hands and still more people are pulling up tourist information, as well as interactive map images and directions out of thin air, as well as news and weather reports.

A recreational park is pulled out of a pocket dimension, for people to enjoy the evening sunshine. Children are soon chatting, laughing, and playing with shapeshifting magic. Eventually, they decide to go somewhere else, so they all change into a variety of birds and fly away, meeting up with another group along the way, doubling the flock size.

The sky overhead grows black, as if it's suddenly been ripped apart to reveal nothingness beyond. Out of that void, comes a Monster. The Monster that killed my mother's parents.

The void-creature casually shoots the flock of birds below him. The children blink out of existence, and the blast continues, uninterrupted. A long travel pod train gets caught in the blast, vanishing as the power strikes the ground, where it leaves a quarter-mile diameter crater. The concert is obliterated. Emergency services respond, but they, too, are caught in the attack. Mages and fighters of all descriptions try to stop the void-creature, but the cannon rips through shields and armour, like they're not there. He must be stopped.

Mandalee and the other Guardians arrive, fighting with Temporal magic, using every bit of skill and power they possess, and at last, something slows the creature down, but even they can't stop it. Temporal shields that could hold back an Angel, buckle under the assault.

Aunt Mandalee finally calls me in – she probably should have called earlier, but she feared for my safety. I can sense the Temporal component of his weapon and try to wrap him in a Time bubble. After experimenting with various harmonic variations, I manage to nullify the Temporal aspect of his blasts. They still cause mass destruction, but I'm hopeful that the Guardians can find ways to undo much of that through some clinical Time Interventions.

At last, the tide of battle turns, and the void-creature slips through a portal. The Guardians are exhausted, but I give chase. I can't let him damage Time, but by that same token, I must be careful – pitched battles between us through Time would make the ancient feud of the shadow warriors look like playground fighting.

He eventually flees somewhere even I cannot go, which should be impossible, but I have come to realise that the rules don't apply to him, because his power comes, in part, from outside the Great Cosmic Sandwich. Somehow, he is channelling the chaotic power of *IT*.

We've been waging a war for over a year since that first day, and we're powerless to do anything more than slow the void-creature down.

If this Monster is not stopped, we'll never need to worry about the void storms, and if he's not stopped quickly, the void storms will make our war magnificently irrelevant.

But where did this Monster come from and where does my desperate and dangerous plan fit into this? Why have I sent Mandalee back in time to fetch my father from the past, and why from that particular moment? To give you those answers, I must continue to hold back Time and keep the Red and Black Guardians from interfering.

Speaking of which, they're giving me some trouble at the moment, and I'm afraid they might just break free if I don't do something to discourage them. So, if you'll excuse me, gentle reader, I shall go and deal with them. Then on my return, I shall tell you the story of how Daelen StormTiger, my father, first met my mother, and everything was set in motion.

A sneak preview of the sequel
to *Shifting Stars*

Gathering Storm

The Salvation of Tempestria
Book 2

Gary Stringer

Available Spring 2021

Chapter 1

The Council of Wizards was in crisis: wizards were going missing.

There was no obvious pattern relating to faction, power, ability or involvement in Council affairs, so there was no way of knowing who might be next.

Exactly when this started, gentle reader, it was difficult to say. Missing people were an unfortunate fact of life, in ways both ordinary and extraordinary, such as demon attack. These disappearances were different, however. It wasn't always possible to determine precisely where they were when they disappeared, but where it was possible, investigations revealed an energy source of higher planar origins.

This was new: beings from the higher planes had never before shown any interest in taking mortals. They were often collateral damage, caught in the crossfire, but never deliberately attacked. If that had changed, and the shadow warriors were now kidnapping innocent Tempestrians for who-knew-what purposes, what could be done about it?

My mother, Catriona, already knew Aunt Dreya's views on the matter. She had shared her intention to kill Daelen StormTiger not long after Cat had moved in, and current events, more than two years later, as the Tempestrian chronometer flies, compelled Catriona to share something that had been puzzling her about it.

"Why Daelen, specifically?" Catriona asked her. "Why not Kullos, or that other one…the dark clone. The one that looks a bit like Daelen but isn't…has anybody heard that one's name, by the way?"

"Not that I know of," Dreya replied. "Anyway, what do you care which one I kill?"

"I don't, especially," Cat shrugged. "They're all about as dangerous as each other, as far as I can tell. They've got no business fighting their war here, and I'd be quite happy to be rid of the lot of them. Which is precisely why I ask the question: Why Daelen, specifically? Why do *you* care which one you kill?"

Dreya frowned. She'd never really questioned it. Daelen was a self-proclaimed Protector and seen as a hero to many, trying to save them from Kullos, who was generally viewed as the villain. Recently, though, there had been growing, popular support for the reverse sentiment. Dreya the Dark agreed with Catriona that there was little basis for either view, but that only further highlighted her question. Surely it wasn't a matter of killing Daelen because of his hero image or because he was famous. Those were not worthy motivations for Dreya the Dark. Yet, something was nagging in her brain, almost like a voice, her own voice, telling her he was the one she should go for. It was important.

'*Kill Daelen StormTiger,*' said the voice, '*and take his power.*'

The voice kept telling her to ignore the reasons why, but that wasn't how Dreya operated. She didn't do random violence. She didn't attack without cause.

"I don't know," she admitted, finally, "and I don't like that I don't know. If I didn't know better, I might suspect some kind of mental attack or a post-hypnotic suggestion, but my shields prevent any such thing."

Her shields were intact. From the day Dreya claimed the Tower, the only magical signature that had ever passed through her defences, apart from Catriona's, was her own. Still, the point was chiefly academic for the foreseeable future. Dreya knew she wasn't ready to take on a being from the higher planes. Not yet. Besides, she didn't even know how to find them if she wanted to. Nobody knew where the shadow warriors went, between battles. Dreya suspected the answer lay on some other world, but her best efforts to probe the cosmos with her magic had so far failed to prove their existence.

"Anyway, it's a moot point at the moment," Dreya told Cat, dismissing the issue. "After all, it's not as if Daelen StormTiger himself is going to come knocking on my door!"

Cat laughed, "That's true."

And so, she let the subject drop.

Returning to their original topic of conversation, Dreya needed to share some news that she knew Catriona was not going to like.

"Cat," she began, "I just came from an emergency Council meeting."

"I know," Cat nodded, "you told me this morning, remember?"

"Yes, but I didn't tell you why it was called."

"About all those wizards disappearing, I presumed."

"Yes, but the situation's got even more serious for your faction in particular, though it affects everyone, really. Cat, I'm sorry to have to tell you this, but the latest wizard to vanish is Mistress Justaria."

For one of the Triumvirate to disappear was a severe blow to the whole magical community. If Daelen or one of his kind were proved to be behind it, that could be seen as nothing less than a declaration of war.

Catriona liked Mistress Justaria. The leader of the Red robes of Balance had been fair-minded at Catriona's Conclave, and the druidess had always taken to heart the conversation they'd shared afterwards. Justaria had been absolutely right that the college was entirely the wrong place for her, and in many ways, her encouragement to seek knowledge elsewhere was a key reason why she was now living and working in the Black Tower. More than that, she felt she owed an enormous debt of thanks to Justaria for her hand in events that had led to her close bond with Dreya the Dark. The chance to see the person behind the mask, the woman beneath the black velvet robes. The opportunity to come to know and understand Dreya in ways no-one else did.

Dreya had visited many of the known disappearance sites herself, but she understood Catriona well enough by now to be completely unsurprised when the druidess declared her intention to investigate this one personally.

*****

A red-banded falcon alighted in Justaria's garden. It wasn't large, but it was well maintained. Flowering plants were blooming in a wide border between the fence and the lawn on the right-hand side as she faced the white cottage at the end of the gently meandering path. Over to the left, the Red robe leader had gone for a different approach, with a blanket of buttercups and daisies encircling a sycamore tree.

Catriona reverted to her natural form and breathed deeply. She could immediately sense the signature of higher planar energy that had got everybody so worked up. But there was something else not quite right about this place. A spell of wizards had been all over Justaria's garden, probing with their magic and in their wizardly wisdom, turned up absolutely nothing.

"Wizards!" the druidess muttered to herself. "Can't see past their own spellbooks!"

She sent a sympathic apology to Dreya, with whom she was linked.

'*Not wrong*,' came her reply.

Barring a few footprints where wizards had trodden carelessly, the garden was beautiful, but not immaculate. It didn't look like a professional job to Cat. More of a constant labour of love. Clearly, Justaria spent a lot of her free time planting, pottering and pruning, tinkering and tidying her garden. So why were the daisies bent over? If they had just been stepped on, why was it just the daisies and not the buttercups? And why all in one direction, towards the tree? Cat stepped lightly around to the far side of the tree where the trunk was in shadow. On the ground was a trowel with a sharp metal point, which had obviously been used to carve words into the bark:

RHYNAS

DESERT

The druidess wasn't sure where that was, apart from being somewhere overseas, but by concentrating hard, she was able to project an image of the words to Dreya, sympathically. In return, Dreya sent '*Meeting*' and '*Map,*' which Cat took to mean she would meet up with her and show her on a map.

Looking around Justaria's garden once more, there was no other evidence that Catriona could detect. It was a wonder the sorceress had found time to do as much as she did. She could almost picture the scene: whoever had come for Justaria, she had found out where they were taking her and delayed them long enough to leave clues.

At her Conclave, Cat had seen Justaria use delicate magic to make a pen inscribe words on a page with barely a glance. In principle, using a floating trowel to scratch words into a tree was no different. As for the daisies, they were just more evidence of Justaria's deft touch with magic. Still, it would have taken time, which told Cat something else: unless Justaria's case was different from all the others, wizards were not being kidnapped as everyone assumed. If it were a simple grab and teleport job, there was no way Justaria could have done what she did. She must have kept them talking, and if they were talking, it wasn't kidnapping, it was persuasion. Recruitment. That said, given the lack of reports of wizards saying 'no' to this recruitment, it was likely the sales pitch boiled down to 'join or die,' but still, recruitment for what?

As she was puzzling over that one, someone arrived who had the answer.

The wind suddenly picked up, and Cat was instantly alert. Storms didn't just start like that. Not natural ones, anyway. There was a flash of equally unnatural lightning, creating an outline of a member of the big cat family: a tiger.

Cat shifted to her tawny owl form, quieter through the air than the falcon, approaching the new arrival stealthily from behind. She changed in midair and stood on one of her Windy Steps.

"Daelen StormTiger," she said, scowling indignantly, arms folded. "What the hell are you doing here?"

GARY STRINGER is the author of the new novel *Shifting Stars*.

Shifting Stars marks the beginning of the epic series, *The Salvation of Tempestria*. A fantasy world within a wider sci-fi universe, populated by bold characters with ridiculous radical ideas, as told by an immortal girl from the future with a plan to save the world...or possibly end it.

Scientist by profession, Gary gives real science concepts a fantasy twist in his writing.

While studying for his B.Sc. in Chemistry, he discovered the fantasy genre and he's barely stopped reading since!

He lives in the seaside town of Blackpool, UK, and enjoys long walks and theme parks in the summer, and theatre shows in the winter.

His previous work includes the *Majaos Trilogy* available from Obooko.com rated 5 stars out of 5 across the 3 books. This work is a decade-long labour of love stemming back to his University days that turns familiar fantasy tropes on their heads.